Gogol's Wife

& Other Stories

Tommaso Landolfi

Gogol's Wife

Translated by Raymond Rosenthal

x Other Stories

hn Longrigg, Wayland Young

New Directions

c.2

Acknowledgments

Wayland Young's translation of "Gogol's Wife" and John Longrigg's translation of "Pastoral" first appeared in *Encounter*, London.

The original Italian titles and volume sources of the stories included in this collection are: from *Dialogo dei massimi sistemi* (Fratelli Parenti Editori, Florence, 1937): "La morte del Re di Francia," "Dialogo dei massimi sistemi"; from *La spada* (Vallecchi Editore, Florence, 1944): "Notte di nozze," "Lettera di un romantico sul giuoco," "Colpo di sole"; from *Le due zittelle* (Bompiani, Milan, 1946): "Le due zittelle"; from *Ombre* (Vallecchi Editore, Florence, 1954): "La moglie di Gogol," "Giovanni e sua moglie," "Lettere dalla provincia." A collected one-volume edition of Landolfi's stories, *Racconti,* was published in 1961 by Vallecchi.

Manufactured in the United States of America.
New Directions Books are published by James Laughlin
at Norfolk, Connecticut. New York Office: 333 Sixth Avenue, 14.

BL

JAN 1 1 '64

Contents

Gogol's Wife

& Other Stories

Gogol's Wife

Nine bizarre stories gathered from "the Italian Kafka's" output of twenty five years.

A T THIS point, confronted with the whole complicated affair of Nikolai Vassilevitch's wife, I am overcome by hesitation. Have I any right to disclose something which is unknown to the whole world, which my unforgettable friend himself kept hidden from the world (and he had his reasons), and which I am sure will give rise to all sorts of malicious and stupid misunderstandings? Something, moreover, which will very probably offend the sensibilities of all sorts of base, hypocritical people, and possibly of some honest people too, if there are any left? And finally, have I any right to disclose something before which my own spirit recoils, and even tends toward a more or less open disapproval?

But the fact remains that, as a biographer, I have certain firm obligations. Believing as I do that every bit of information about so lofty a genius will turn out to be of value to us and to future generations, I cannot conceal something which in any case has no hope of being judged fairly and wisely until the end of time. Moreover, what right have we to condemn? Is it given to us to know, not only what intimate needs, but even what higher and wider ends may have been served by those very deeds of a lofty genius which perchance may appear to us vile? No indeed, for we understand so little of these privileged natures. "It is true," a great man once said, "that I also have to pee, but for quite different reasons."

But without more ado I will come to what I know beyond doubt, and can prove beyond question, about this controversial matter, which will now—I dare to hope—no longer be so. I will not trouble to recapitulate what is already known of it, since I do not think this should be necessary at the present stage of development of Gogol studies.

Let me say it at once: Nikolai Vassilevitch's wife was not a woman. Nor was she any sort of human being, nor any sort of living creature at all, whether animal or vegetable (although something of the sort has sometimes been hinted). She was quite simply a balloon. Yes, a balloon; and this will explain the perplexity, or even indignation, of certain biographers who were also the personal friends of the Master, and who complained that, although they often went to his house, they never saw her and "never even heard her voice." From this they deduced all sorts of dark and disgraceful complications—yes, and criminal ones too. No, gentlemen, everything is always simpler than it appears. You did not hear her voice simply because she could not speak, or to be more exact, she could only speak in certain conditions, as we shall see. And it was always, except once, in tête-à-tête with Nikolai Vassilevitch. So let us not waste time with any cheap or empty refutations but come at once to as exact and complete a description as possible of the being or object in question.

Gogol's so-called wife was an ordinary dummy made of thick rubber, naked at all seasons, buff in tint, or as is more commonly said, flesh-colored. But since women's skins are not all of the same color, I should specify that hers was a light-colored, polished skin, like that of certain brunettes. It, or she, was, it is hardly necessary to add, of feminine sex. Perhaps I should say at once that she was capable of very wide alterations of her attributes without, of course, being able to alter her sex itself. She could sometimes appear to be thin, with hardly any breasts and with narrow hips more like a young lad than a woman, and at other times to be excessively well-endowed or—let us not mince matters—fat. And she often changed the color of her hair, both on her head and elsewhere on her body, though not necessarily at the same time. She could also seem to change in all sorts of other tiny particulars, such as the position of moles, the vitality of the mucous membranes and so forth. She could even to a certain extent change the very color of her skin. One is faced with the necessity of asking oneself who she really was, or whether it would be proper to speak of a single "person"—and in fact we shall see that it would be imprudent to press this point.

The cause of these changes, as my readers will already have understood, was nothing else but the will of Nikolai Vassilevitch himself. He would inflate her to a greater or lesser degree, would change her wig and her other tufts of hair, would grease her with ointments and touch her up in various ways so as to obtain more or less the type of woman which suited him at that moment. Following the natural inclinations of his fancy, he even amused himself sometimes by producing grotesque or monstrous forms; as will be readily understood, she became deformed when inflated beyond a certain point or if she remained below a certain pressure.

But Gogol soon tired of these experiments, which he held to be "after all, not very respectful" to his wife, whom he loved in his own way—however inscrutable it may remain to us. He loved her, but which of these incarnations, we may ask ourselves, did he love? Alas, I have already indicated that the end of the present account will furnish some sort of an answer. And how can I have stated above that it was Nikolai Vassilevitch's will which ruled that woman? In a certain sense, yes, it is true; but it is equally certain that she soon became no longer his slave but his tyrant. And here yawns the abyss, or if you prefer it, the Jaws of Tartarus. But let us not anticipate.

I have said that Gogol obtained with his manipulations *more or less* the type of woman which he needed from time to time. I should add that when, in rare cases, the form he obtained perfectly incarnated his desire, Nikolai Vassilevitch fell in love with it "exclusively," as he said in his own words, and that this was enough to render "her" stable for a certain time—until he fell out of love with "her." I counted no more than three or four of these violent passions—or, as I suppose they would be called today, infatuations—in the life (dare I say in the conjugal life?) of the great writer. It will be convenient to add here that a few years after what one may call his marriage, Gogol had even given a name to his wife. It was Caracas, which is, unless I am mistaken, the capital of Venezuela. I have never been able to discover the reason for this choice: great minds are so capricious!

Speaking only of her normal appearance, Caracas was what is called a fine woman—well built and proportioned in every part. She had every smallest attribute of her sex properly disposed in the proper location. Particularly worthy of attention were her genital organs (if the adjective is permissible in such a context). They were formed by means of ingenious folds in the rubber. Nothing was forgotten, and their operation was rendered easy by various devices, as well as by the internal pressure of the air.

Caracas also had a skeleton, even though a rudimentary one. Perhaps it was made of whalebone. Special care had been devoted to the construction of the thoracic cage, of the pelvic basin and of the cranium. The first two systems were more or less visible in accordance with the thickness of the fatty layer, if I may so describe it, which covered them. It is a great pity that Gogol never let me know the name of the creator of such a fine piece of work. There was an obstinacy in his refusal which was never quite clear to me.

Nikolai Vassilevitch blew his wife up through the anal sphincter with a pump of his own invention, rather like those which you hold down with your two feet and which are used today in all sorts of mechanical workshops. Situated in the anus was a little one-way valve, or whatever the correct technical description would be, like the mitral valve of the heart, which, once the body was inflated, allowed more air to come in but none to go out. To deflate, one unscrewed a stopper in the mouth, at the back of the throat.

And that, I think, exhausts the description of the most

noteworthy peculiarities of this being. Unless perhaps I should mention the splendid rows of white teeth which adorned her mouth and the dark eyes which, in spite of their immobility, perfectly simulated life. Did I say simulate? Good heavens, simulate is not the word! Nothing seems to be the word, when one is speaking of Caracas! Even these eyes could undergo a change of color, by means of a special process to which, since it was long and tiresome, Gogol seldom had recourse. Finally, I should speak of her voice, which it was only once given to me to hear. But I cannot do that without going more fully into the relationship between husband and wife, and in this I shall no longer be able to answer to the truth of everything with absolute certitude. On my conscience I could not—so confused, both in itself and in my memory, is that which I now have to tell.

Here, then, as they occur to me, are some of my memories.

The first and, as I said, the last time I ever heard Caracas speak to Nikolai Vassilevitch was one evening when we were absolutely alone. We were in the room where the woman, if I may be allowed the expression, lived. Entrance to this room was strictly forbidden to everybody. It was furnished more or less in the Oriental manner, had no windows and was situated in the most inaccessible part of the house. I did know that she could talk, but Gogol had never explained to me the circumstances under which this happened. There were only the two of us, or three, in there. Nikolai Vassilevitch and I were drinking vodka and discussing Butkov's novel. I remember that we left this topic, and he was maintaining the necessity for radical reforms in the laws of inheritance. We had almost forgotten her. It was then that, with a husky and submissive voice, like Venus on the nuptial couch, she said point-blank: "I want to go poo poo."

I jumped, thinking I had misheard, and looked across at her. She was sitting on a pile of cushions against the wall; that evening she was a soft, blonde beauty, rather well-covered. Her expression seemed commingled of shrewdness and slyness, childishness and irresponsibility. As for Gogol, he blushed violently and, leaping on her, stuck two fingers down her throat. She immediately began to shrink and to turn pale; she took on once again that lost and astonished air which was especially hers, and was in the end reduced to no more than a flabby skin on a perfunctory bony armature. Since, for practical reasons which will readily be divined, she had an extraordinarily flexible backbone, she folded up almost in two, and for the rest of the evening she looked up at us from where she had slithered to the floor, in utter abjection.

All Gogol said was: "She only does it for a joke, or to annoy me, because as a matter of fact she does not have such needs." In the presence of other people, that is to say of me, he generally made a point of treating her with a certain disdain.

We went on drinking and talking, but Nikolai Vassilevitch seemed very much disturbed and absent in spirit. Once he suddenly interrupted what he was saying, seized my hand in his and burst into tears. "What can I do now?" he exclaimed. "You understand, Foma Paskalovitch, that I loved her?"

It is necessary to point out that it was impossible, except by a miracle, ever to repeat any of Caracas' forms. She was a fresh creation every time, and it would have been wasted effort to seek to find again the exact proportions, the exact pressure,

and so forth, of a former Caracas. Therefore the plumpish
blonde of that evening was lost to Gogol from that time forth
forever; this was in fact the tragic end of one of those few loves of
Nikolai Vassilevitch, which I described above. He gave me no
explanation; he sadly rejected my proffered comfort, and that
evening we parted early. But his heart had been laid bare to me
in that outburst. He was no longer so reticent with me, and soon
had hardly any secrets left. And this, I may say in parenthesis,
caused me very great pride.

It seems that things had gone well for the "couple" at
the beginning of their life together. Nikolai Vassilevitch had
been content with Caracas and slept regularly with her in the
same bed. He continued to observe this custom till the end, saying with a timid smile that no companion could be quieter or
less importunate than she. But I soon began to doubt this, especially judging by the state he was sometimes in when he
woke up. Then, after several years, their relationship began
strangely to deteriorate.

All this, let it be said once and for all, is no more than a
schematic attempt at an explanation. About that time the
woman actually began to show signs of independence or, as one
might say, of autonomy. Nikolai Vassilevitch had the extraordinary impression that she was acquiring a personality of her own,
indecipherable perhaps, but still distinct from his, and one
which slipped through his fingers. It is certain that some sort of
continuity was established between each of her appearances—
between all those brunettes, those blondes, those redheads and
auburn-headed girls, between those plump, those slim, those
dusky or snowy or golden beauties, there was a certain some-

thing in common. At the beginning of this chapter I cast some doubt on the propriety of considering Caracas as a unitary personality; nevertheless I myself could not quite, whenever I saw her, free myself of the impression that, however unheard of it may seem, this was fundamentally the same woman. And it may be that this was why Gogol felt he had to give her a name.

An attempt to establish in what precisely subsisted the common attributes of the different forms would be quite another thing. Perhaps it was no more and no less than the creative afflatus of Nikolai Vassilevitch himself. But no, it would have been too singular and strange if he had been so much divided off from himself, so much averse to himself. Because whoever she was, Caracas was a disturbing presence and even—it is better to be quite clear—a hostile one. Yet neither Gogol nor I ever succeeded in formulating a remotely tenable hypothesis as to her true nature; when I say formulate, I mean in terms which would be at once rational and accessible to all. But I cannot pass over an extraordinary event which took place at this time.

Caracas fell ill of a shameful disease—or rather Gogol did—though he was not then having, nor had he ever had, any contact with other women. I will not even try to describe how this happened, or where the filthy complaint came from; all I know is that it happened. And that my great, unhappy friend would say to me: "So, Foma Paskalovitch, you see what lay at the heart of Caracas; it was the spirit of syphilis."

Sometimes he would even blame himself in a quite absurd manner; he was always prone to self-accusation. This incident was a real catastrophe as far as the already obscure relationship between husband and wife, and the hostile feelings of Nikolai

Vassilevitch himself, were concerned. He was compelled to undergo long-drawn-out and painful treatment—the treatment of those days—and the situation was aggravated by the fact that the disease in the woman did not seem to be easily curable. Gogol deluded himself for some time that, by blowing his wife up and down and furnishing her with the most widely divergent aspects, he could obtain a woman immune from the contagion, but he was forced to desist when no results were forthcoming.

I shall be brief, seeking not to tire my readers, and also because what I remember seems to become more and more confused. I shall therefore hasten to the tragic conclusion. As to this last, however, let there be no mistake. I must once again make it clear that I am very sure of my ground. I was an eyewitness. Would that I had not been!

The years went by. Nikolai Vassilevitch's distaste for his wife became stronger, though his love for her did not show any signs of diminishing. Toward the end, aversion and attachment struggled so fiercely with each other in his heart that he became quite stricken, almost broken up. His restless eyes, which habitually assumed so many different expressions and sometimes spoke so sweetly to the heart of his interlocutor, now almost always shone with a fevered light, as if he were under the effect of a drug. The strangest impulses arose in him, accompanied by the most senseless fears. He spoke to me of Caracas more and more often, accusing her of unthinkable and amazing things. In these regions I could not follow him, since I had but a sketchy acquaintance with his wife, and hardly any intimacy—and above all since my sensibility was so limited compared with his. I shall accordingly restrict myself to reporting some of his accusations, without reference to my personal impressions.

"Believe it or not, Foma Paskalovitch," he would, for example, often say to me: "Believe it or not, *she's aging!*" Then, unspeakably moved, he would, as was his way, take my hands in his. He also accused Caracas of giving herself up to solitary pleasures, which he had expressly forbidden. He even went so far as to charge her with betraying him, but the things he said became so extremely obscure that I must excuse myself from any further account of them.

One thing that appears certain is that toward the end Caracas, whether aged or not, had turned into a bitter creature, querulous, hypocritical and subject to religious excess. I do not exclude the possibility that she may have had an influence on Gogol's moral position during the last period of his life, a position which is sufficiently well known. The tragic climax came one night quite unexpectedly when Nikolai Vassilevitch and I were celebrating his silver wedding—one of the last evenings we were to spend together. I neither can nor should attempt to set down what it was that led to his decision, at a time when to all appearances he was resigned to tolerating his consort. I know not what new events had taken place that day. I shall confine myself to the facts; my readers must make what they can of them.

That evening Nikolai Vassilevitch was unusually agitated. His distaste for Caracas seemed to have reached an unprecedented intensity. The famous "pyre of vanities"—the burning of his manuscripts—had already taken place; I should not like to say whether or not at the instigation of his wife. His state of mind had been further inflamed by other causes. As to his physi-

cal condition, this was ever more pitiful, and strengthened my
impression that he took drugs. All the same, he began to talk in
a more or less normal way about Belinsky, who was giving him
some trouble with his attacks on the *Selected Correspondence*.
Then suddenly, tears rising to his eyes, he interrupted himself
and cried out: "No. No. It's too much, too much. I can't go on
any longer," as well as other obscure and disconnected phrases
which he would not clarify. He seemed to be talking to himself.
He wrung his hands, shook his head, got up and sat down again
after having taken four or five anxious steps round the room.
When Caracas appeared, or rather when we went in to her later
in the evening in her Oriental chamber, he controlled himself
no longer and began to behave like an old man, if I may so
express myself, in his second childhood, quite giving way to his
absurd impulses. For instance, he kept nudging me and winking
and senselessly repeating: "There she is, Foma Paskalovitch;
there she is!" Meanwhile she seemed to look up at us with a
disdainful attention. But behind these "mannerisms" one could
feel in him a real repugnance, a repugnance which had, I suppose, now reached the limits of the endurable. Indeed . . .

After a certain time Nikolai Vassilevitch seemed to pluck
up courage. He burst into tears, but somehow they were more
manly tears. He wrung his hands again, seized mine in his, and
walked up and down, muttering: "That's enough! We can't
have any more of this. This is an unheard of thing. How can
such a thing be happening to me? How can a man be expected
to put up with *this?*"

He then leapt furiously upon the pump, the existence of
which he seemed just to have remembered, and, with it in his

hand, dashed like a whirlwind to Caracas. He inserted the tube in her anus and began to inflate her. . . . Weeping the while, he shouted like one possessed: "Oh, how I love her, how I love her, my poor, poor darling! . . . But she's going to burst! Unhappy Caracas, most pitiable of God's creatures! But die she must!"

Caracas was swelling up. Nikolai Vassilevitch sweated, wept and pumped. I wished to stop him but, I know not why, I had not the courage. She began to become deformed and shortly assumed the most monstrous aspect; and yet she had not given any signs of alarm—she was used to these jokes. But when she began to feel unbearably full, or perhaps when Nikolai Vassilevitch's intentions became plain to her, she took on an expression of bestial amazement, even a little beseeching, but still without losing that disdainful look. She was afraid, she was even committing herself to his mercy, but still she could not believe in the immediate approach of her fate; she could not believe in the frightful audacity of her husband. He could not see her face because he was behind her. But I looked at her with fascination, and did not move a finger.

At last the internal pressure came through the fragile bones at the base of her skull, and printed on her face an indescribable rictus. Her belly, her thighs, her lips, her breasts and what I could see of her buttocks had swollen to incredible proportions. All of a sudden she belched, and gave a long hissing groan; both these phenomena one could explain by the increase in pressure, which had suddenly forced a way out through the valve in her throat. Then her eyes bulged frantically, threatening to jump out of their sockets. Her ribs flared wide apart and were no longer attached to the sternum, and she resembled a python digesting a donkey. A donkey, did I say? An ox! An elephant! At this point I believed her already dead, but Nikolai Vassilevitch, sweating, weeping and repeating: "My dearest! My beloved! My best!" continued to pump.

She went off unexpectedly and, as it were, all of a piece. It was not one part of her skin which gave way and the rest which followed, but her whole surface at the same instant. She scattered in the air. The pieces fell more or less slowly, according to their size, which was in no case above a very restricted one. I distinctly remember a piece of her cheek, with some lip attached, hanging on the corner of the mantelpiece. Nikolai Vassilevitch stared at me like a madman. Then he pulled himself together and, once more with furious determination, he began carefully to collect those poor rags which once had been the shining skin of Caracas, and all of her.

"Good-by, Caracas," I thought I heard him murmur, "Good-by! You were too pitiable!" And then suddenly and quite audibly: "The fire! The fire! She too must end up in the fire." He crossed himself—with his left hand, of course. Then, when he had picked up all those shriveled rags, even climbing on the furniture so as not to miss any, he threw them straight on the fire in the hearth, where they began to burn slowly and with an excessively unpleasant smell. Nikolai Vassilevitch, like all Russians, had a passion for throwing important things in the fire.

Red in the face, with an inexpressible look of despair, and yet of sinister triumph too, he gazed on the pyre of those miserable remains. He had seized my arm and was squeezing it convulsively. But those traces of what had once been a being were hardly well alight when he seemed yet again to pull himself together, as if he were suddenly remembering something or taking a painful decision. In one bound he was out of the room.

A few seconds later I heard him speaking to me through the door in a broken, plaintive voice: "Foma Paskalovitch, I want you to promise not to look. *Golubchik,* promise not to look at me when I come in."

I don't know what I answered, or whether I tried to reassure him in any way. But he insisted, and I had to promise him, as if he were a child, to hide my face against the wall and only turn round when he said I might. The door then opened violently and Nikolai Vassilevitch burst into the room and ran to the fireplace.

And here I must confess my weakness, though I consider it justified by the extraordinary circumstances. I looked round before Nikolai Vassilevitch told me I could; it was stronger than me. I was just in time to see him carrying something in his arms, something which he threw on the fire with all the rest, so that it suddenly flared up. At that, since the desire to *see* had entirely mastered every other thought in me, I dashed to the fireplace. But Nikolai Vassilevitch placed himself between me and it and pushed me back with a strength of which I had not believed him capable. Meanwhile the object was burning and giving off clouds of smoke. And before he showed any sign of calming down there was nothing left but a heap of silent ashes.

The true reason why I wished to see was because I had already glimpsed. But it was only a glimpse, and perhaps I should not allow myself to introduce even the slightest element of uncertainty into this true story. And yet, an eyewitness account is not complete without a mention of that which the witness knows with less than complete certainty. To cut a long story short, that something was a baby. Not a flesh and blood baby, of course, but more something in the line of a rubber doll or a model. Something, which, to judge by its appearance, could have been called *Caracas' son.*

Was I mad too? That I do not know, but I do know that this was what I saw, not clearly, but with my own eyes. And I wonder why it was that when I was writing this just now I didn't mention that when Nikolai Vassilevitch came back into the room he was muttering between his clenched teeth: "Him too! Him too!"

And that is the sum of my knowledge of Nikolai Vassilevitch's wife. In the next chapter I shall tell what happened to him afterwards, and that will be the last chapter of his life. But to give an interpretation of his feelings for his wife, or indeed for anything, is quite another and more difficult matter, though I have attempted it elsewhere in this volume, and refer the reader to that modest effort. I hope I have thrown sufficient light on a most controversial question and that I have unveiled the mystery, if not of Gogol, then at least of his wife. In the course of this I have implicitly given the lie to the insensate accusation that he ill-treated or even beat his wife, as well as other like absurdities. And what else can be the goal of a humble biographer such as the present writer but to serve the memory of that lofty genius who is the object of his study?

Translated by Wayland Young

Pastoral

DEAREST Solange:

You were utterly mistaken. I have waited till now, till I was quite certain, before telling you so; and now I can tell you in all honesty—"I can *really* tell you" as the worthy Madame de Caulaincourt puts it. To imagine that I could not bear to live here for longer than a week! Solange, this is heaven on earth. And think of this: I have been here for nearly two months. If you only knew, my dearest, how I bless the inspiration that brought me to this place—my uncle's inspiration, too, in doing his duty by dying at the right time. Say what you will, my uncertain budget was hardly aided by the Empress's balls, or by my frequent visits to the Palais Royal. Here, the delightful and the sensible are united. I taste, for example, the pleasures of possessions—or rather, of property—in a way impossible with Parisian bankers, who do what they please with your money when they

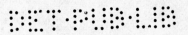

see that you know nothing of finance. In any case, I cannot leave everything in the hands of the agent here. I do not wish to speak ill of my late uncle's régime; but the agent has already bought himself two houses in the village, and a piece of land in the neighborhood. But I did not mean to speak of this matter; and it is certainly not for this reason that I bless my resoultion. My poor Solange, how can you know, how can I tell you, of the unsullied joys of country life, of this delicious new world?

In short, picture me, the happy mistress of a real castle and of a large estate—and the conscientious administrator of the latter. I often wander in my carriage through my woods, which the autumn is already beginning to touch with gold. I often go to the village, which, I may add, also belongs to me, with its simple inhabitants (the agent's affairs are in hand). I confess that the carriage creaks a little; and that the coachman and his groom have not the philosophical air and the carefully cultivated mustaches of their Parisian colleagues—and I cannot understand a word they say. But, by way of compensation, their liveries are far more attractive.

Paris! Of course I will return there sometimes, perhaps often. But—dare I say it?—the whole world of Paris now seems to me like a bad dream.

You should not think that I am afflicted by solitude. The more or less noble landowners of the district have hastened to call on me; most of them, of course, are insupportably provincial, stupid and bigoted. But among them there is one . . . a man who . . . I might as well speak plainly. He is young, dashing, romantic. He rides like an Englishman. He reads the poets and recites them ardently . . . well, why not? After all, he bears one

of the oldest names of the region. Like me, he is free and independent. But I can hear you ask, "What do you mean: why
not?" Well, my love, I can tell you no more of this now.

This letter has already continued too long. Will you have
time, I wonder, between your entertainments and balls to read
it? Certainly not to meditate over it; nor dare I hope that you
will be able to tear yourself for a few days away from the mael-
strom of your life in Paris and allow me to embrace you again.
Farewell, then, I will send you more news of me very soon.

Anne

2

Darling Solange, it is I. So much time has passed since we
met, and even since we last corresponded. But I have had so
many and such pleasant things to do.

Very well, you want to know how the people here start to
hibernate at the beginning of winter—and we are almost there.
It is easily said: they do nothing in particular; they make no
preparations—except a solemn feast, with appropriate potations,
the day before they settle down. There are no *lits embaumés,* no
ointments, no purging of blood or vapors, no injections, no at-
tendants, no fussy quarantine, none of the many operations
usual at our (but now I should say "your") *maisons de léthargie.*
And without any of this things seem to go excellently by
themselves—though you would find it hard to convince the
Paris specialists! And do you know where they hibernate?

Certainly not in "carefully conditioned surroundings," or wrapped in a "softly reacting substance which . . ." etc., etc., but simply where they happen to be, or where they will—in the kitchen, perhaps, or the hayloft—wrapped in a goatskin, of the kind they use for wineskins or bagpipes. More precisely, it seems that they have themselves suspended, or suspend themselves, from beams in the ceiling—and so good night! I have in fact seen, a few days ago, some of these goatskins, or rather bags made of skins (for one skin would not be enough for a child), hanging from a beam, when I was visiting a large and needy family. They were empty, of course; but their use was explained to me. The hairy side is turned inward, and, at one extremity, there is an extension for the legs. In these bags they remain seated, or almost so; so that, with the softer parts of their bodies weighing down, they hang there like so many kitchen vessels. I will give you further details of this, for I feel that it will not be long before the hibernation begins. Another thing: the number of people in Paris who hibernate is severely limited—for all I know, negligible. Indeed, among us (I mean, among you) nobody hibernates except those who are so poor that they have not even a dry crust to eat, or some old general in retirement, or some hysterical woman who cannot bear the cold, and so on. But here the practice is by far more common and extends even to the young, even to children.

Well, we will see. I will keep you informed; but I have nothing more of interest to tell you now. Remember me.

A

3

Dear Solange:

The winter is advancing with giant strides, indeed it has already arrived in these parts; and the people here are beginning to hibernate. I can no longer keep count of the bags hanging from the beams during my visits of charity. They—the bags, I mean—give off a foetid odor like bladders of lard, and soot is already gathering on their surface, for they are nearly all in the kitchens. The spectacle is certainly repellent—but, above all, surprising. Besides I must timidly confess that I have never before seen a human being hibernating. Yes, yes, I know that you will laugh at me; after being very wise about it in my last letter, I now remember that, at one time in Paris, the practice was quite fashionable among unhappy lovers (who even tried to prolong the period of insensibility indefinitely); so that one who has ever been a woman of the world should almost feel ashamed not to be minutely informed about it. But, with humility, I repeat that I had never seen a human being hibernating. In truth one cannot be said to see them hibernating here, since they hang like blocks of wood; one cannot even hear them breathe. How strange these people are, who do not hesitate to subtract the entire winter from their span of life!

In my admitted ignorance, I wonder whether this practice is really a practice, in the sense of a habit? Or whether it is in some way connected with the nature of these people and of all those, in general, given to hibernation? Or is it a habit which has become second nature to them? I do not know what to think, or even, as you see, how to frame the question properly. If we are to judge by the unhappy lovers of Paris, we may conclude that hibernation is a voluntary action; and yet. . . . But why do I burden myself with these reflections . . . unless it is another consequence of living here? In any case, listen to this.

A few days ago I saw, in one of the poor houses, a tiny and charming little boy, whom I already knew—one of my little friends, in fact. They were preparing him for hibernation. He was yawning and rubbing his eyes, and did not seem in the least discontented. But I could not bear the thought that four or five months of that young life would be thrown away. I spoke to the family and told them that I was prepared to take him with me for the winter. I meant not only that I would relieve them of a mouth to feed, but also that I would try to keep him awake and maintain his interest in life. They only understood part of my meaning. The little boy was consulted; he mumbled something indistinct but did not seem to oppose my suggestion. To cut a long story short, I took him with me to the castle. It would be quite useless to try to describe to you the efforts which I made to keep him lively and in good spirits, or even awake—I mean, literally, awake. I failed completely. Nothing amused him, nothing interested him; he yawned continually and seemed to desire nothing but to fall asleep. Indeed he did go to sleep all over the house, in my arms when I was talking to him, while he was eating the rarest delicacies. And he was by no means a stupid child, as I had been able to observe before this languor had overcome him. In the end, I had to take him back, sound asleep, to his family, who, with a smile hinting that they had expected no other outcome, returned him without further ado into his bag—and added: "Shall we talk about it again—in April?"

Well, what do you say to that? Ah, why do you write to me so seldom? Why do you tell me nothing of Paris and of your life? Do you think that I have become altogether a savage? Farewell—write to me soon.

A

4

Solange, my dear:

I begin to be alarmed; I can no longer hide it either from myself or from you. An unbelievable number of people here have already fallen asleep. Wherever I go, I see nothing but hideous, foetid bags hanging from the ceilings. And one incident sums it up. Do you remember that in my first letter I spoke of a noble and romantic young man who . . . who was paying his addresses to me? Very well then, he—yes, he . . . oh, Solange! Yesterday we were in my drawing room. I had played a little. He, in his turn, had recited a poem, written by himself, whose inspiration only modesty prevents me from revealing to you. The hour was propitious for our hearts to declare themselves. I was at that very moment thinking that the time had come when I could give him some grounds for hope, that there was no reason in the world why I should not do so. He had seized my hand, and I had abandoned it to him, when . . . ah, my friend, how can I tell you? Behind his gaze, I saw with horror the beginning of a sort of languor, not of the kind you would have imagined, but terribly like a sort of dullness, even of indifference—the indifference of a man who is on the point of falling asleep. Think, Solange, at that very moment of all moments he was beginning to fall asleep! For a little while he held my hand in his, doing nothing, gazing at me ever more childishly, apparently oblivious of our critical conjuncture and of everything else. Then he drew back a little, dropped my poor damp hand, yawned (still, I confess, with urbanity), walked to the window, tapped on the glass, protested something about a headache, mumbled something else incomprehensible, and, without even taking his leave (I was too dismayed to speak) took to his heels. This is the whole story. Today I am told that he has started to hibernate. Oh, no doubt his bag will be made of sables. My God! What else can I say but "My God"?

And the others! I do not remember if I have ever spoken to you about certain of my relations, or rather my uncle's relations. I went to call on them last evening, in part to recover my spirits. I found them all seated around a table, in solemn silence. One glanced occasionally at a newspaper thrown on the table; but not so much at the newspaper as at the advertisements in it. Another was smoking a cigar and staring at his nails; but he was not smoking it so much as occasionally lighting it. A third had his elbows on the table and was doing nothing whatever.

They were silent, or spoke with difficulty of the weather. At the back of their eyes I could see that languor which I have come to recognize. It is not difficult to prophesy that soon they will all have fallen sound asleep.

Meanwhile, this morning a terrified procession of peasants paraded before me, having insisted on seeing me, carrying presents in kind. I was given a confused explanation to the effect that these offerings were always, by tradition, made on this day of the year, and were "for hibernation"—though it is given a different name here. A terrible suspicion crossed my mind: did my uncle hibernate as well? And, in truth, I seem to remember that he used to wait till the spring before answering my winter letters, though he was so precise in all his other dealings. But no! What am I imagining? And yet I recently discovered in the cellar—which I had never visited—an entire store of the horrible bags, and some already full! It seemed to me that I had not seen certain of the servants for some days. But the agent is as lively as ever, and the old butler holds up well, although he is always somewhat dull by nature; and the same may be said of the first housemaid. But the cook has for some time. . . .

But tell me, Solange: do you think it possible that they will all fall asleep? They all tell me—all the survivors, that is—that those who have work to do remain awake. But what advice could you give me in such a matter?

The snow has fallen in profusion and blankets the fields as far as the eye can reach. It is beautiful, but it is a little sad.

What are you doing in Paris? Will you at last make up your mind to write to me? But in Paris, at this very hour, the carriages are beginning to draw up to the Opera; bejewelled beauties cast their glances to left and to right; their lovers ap-

proach them closely at the entrance; everything in Paris lives
and trembles with movement, the very air trembles.

Ah! Do you think that I ache with nostalgia for all that?
You would be mistaken. It is only my nerves playing a treacher-
ous game with me. I must be resolute—I have sworn to be
resolute. Farewell.

A

5

Solange:

My Solange, my only friend, listen to me, you must save
me now, instantly. The very instant that you receive these lines
you must take your traveling carriage; you must run, you must
fly to save me. Solange, do you love me? Dear God, I cannot
write calmly. I can hear his horse trampling and snorting in the
courtyard below me—I mean the hussar's horse. Yes, they have
all fallen asleep, every last one, in the castle, in the village,
everywhere, all of them. Even the agent, even the old butler a
few hours ago. He was the only one left, and I could find no
way of keeping him awake—with brandy or with offers of
money; he did his best, but in the end it was stronger than he. I
have no time to tell you. I sped outside: the silent desert of the
snow. It was like a fairy tale—no, there is always a kindliness
about fairy tales; it seemed liked a fearful nightmare . . . but I
am wasting precious time, and his horse is trampling ever more

loudly. At last, after an infinite time, I saw him far, far away in the snow, a speck of black which swiftly grew larger. It was a handsome young hussar—he whom, for whatever reason, the Lord has sent me. He was galloping madly. He stopped unwillingly. I begged him, I implored him to carry me with him on the saddle. He replied, "I am carrying orders, Mademoiselle." If you knew what I had to do and to say to induce him to delay for ten minutes, not more than ten minutes (and he took out his watch), just the time to write to you these despairing lines, which he has promised on his honor to have delivered to you by the swiftest means. There are only two minutes left. Understand me well, Solange. I cannot prepare my food, I cannot do anything, there is nothing in the house, I am frightened of the horses, I could not ride them to safety—even if they too are not asleep. I shall die here if you do not save me. Solange, Solange, do you hate me? Yes, you were right after all, but now there is not an instant to lose. . . and if . . . if anything should happen to him on the road? Great heavens, I hear his voice calling me. . . Solange, my soul, what can I say to you? Save your wretched

A

Translated by John Longrigg

Dialogue on the
Greater Harmonies

IN THE morning when we rise from bed, although surprised to find ourselves still alive, we are no less amazed that everything is exactly as we had left it the evening before. Thus I happened to be staring in stupid abstraction through my window curtains when my friend Y announced himself with a series of hasty knocks rapped out on the door of my room.

I knew him for a shy and touchy man devoted to strange studies performed in solitude and mystery, like rituals. Thus I was not a little astounded to observe that day that he was gripped by great excitement. As I dressed and we spoke of inconsequential matters, he passed with extraordinary rapidity from the deepest dejection to a gaiety which seemed to me fictitious. It required no great effort on my part to realize that something unusual or terrible must have happened to him. When, at last, I was ready to listen to him, he told me a strange tale which, for simplicity's sake, I shall report in the first person. He stipulated that, no matter how strange or futile what he was about to say might seem to me, I should not interrupt him—he would be as brief as possible. Stunned and curious, I agreed to his stipulation.

"Well, I must tell you," Y began, "that years ago I dedicated my time to a patient and minute distillation of the elements which compose the work of art. By this path I reached the precise and incontrovertible conclusion that having at his disposal rich and varied expressive means is, for an artist, anything but a favorable circumstance. For instance, it is in my opinion far preferable to write in an imperfectly known language than in one which is absolutely familiar. Even if I do not wish to retrace the involuted and tortuous path which I followed at that time to attain so simple a discovery, this discovery still seems to me today supported by certain self-evident arguments. Quite obviously, anyone who does not know the right words to indicate objects or feelings, is forced to replace them with circumlocutions, that is with images—with what great advantage to art, I leave it to you to imagine. Thus, when technical terms and clichés are avoided, what else can obstruct the birth of a work of art?"

At this point Y, probably satisfied with his reasoning, stopped a moment to gaze at me through partly closed eyes, forgetting his troubles. But noticing my half stupefied, half questioning expression, he sighed and quickly resumed.

"Having reached the conclusion of which I have told you, I stumbled on a monster—there is no other way to put it—a monster of an English captain. You will soon understand why I call him a monster. Oh Lord, why did you not spare me from this curse? Because now I have forever lost my peace! This person was a flabby looking man. He used to eat in my *trattoria* and boasted loudly of his innumerable adventures to a large circle of hangers-on who almost constantly surrounded him. He had been in the Orient for any number of years, and knew a great many Oriental languages—at least, that's what he said. But he boasted particularly of his knowledge of Persian and often shuffled out three or four strange sounds under the nose of the waiter, who stood there blinking his eyes, dumbfounded. It then transpired that he had meant to order a glass of wine or a grilled steak. As you can understand, I loathed this man and yet he managed to get on speaking terms with me and, one sad day, offered to teach me Persian. Eager to test on myself the felicity of my theory, I ended by accepting. My idea, as you'll already have understood, was to learn that language imperfectly: enough to express myself, but not enough always to call things by their right names. Our lessons went forward without a hitch. . .but why can't I resist the temptation to tell you all the noisome details of this story? . . .and I made rapid progress in the new language. According to the captain, one must learn languages by practice: therefore I never laid eyes on a Persian text—besides, it would have been difficult to procure one. To make up for this, during the walks I took with my teacher we spoke only that language and when, tired out, we sat down in some café, the white sheets before us were immediately covered with strange, minute signs. In this manner I spent more than a year: near the end the captain never wearied of praising me highly for the facility with which I had profited from his teaching. One day he announced that he would soon leave, I believe for Scotland, to which place he made off and where, I hope, he has met with the merited desserts for his misdeeds. Since that day I have never seen him."

My friend Y fell silent again, as though mastering his emotions: the distress of the memory coagulated on his face in a painful grimace. Finally he made an effort and continued:

"But by then I knew enough to take up my experiment and that is what I did with the greatest possible ardor. I made it a rule to write only in Persian, though I confined it to the secret outbursts of my soul, to my poetry! Since that time, until a month ago, I wrote my poetry only in Persian. Fortunately, I am not a very fertile poet and the entire production of this period is limited to three brief compositions which I shall show you. In Persian."

I could see that the thought of having written in Persian was unbearable to Y, though I did not yet know why.

"In Persian," Y repeated. "But the moment has come, my poor friend, to explain to you what kind of a language that execrable captain had baptized with the name of Persian. A month ago I was suddenly seized by a desire to read in the original a certain Persian poet—you don't know him—for in reading a poet there is never the danger of learning a language too well. I prepared for the task by again studying attentively the notes taken with the captain, and I had the definite feeling that I could manage it. After much trouble, I finally succeeded in obtaining the text that I wanted. I remember that I received it carefully wrapped in tissue paper. Full of trepidation over this first encounter, I hastened home, lit my small stove and a cigarette, adjusted the lamp in such a way that it threw a bright light on the precious book, settled in my armchair and unwrapped the package.

"My first supposition was that there had been a mistake: the signs there before my eyes had nothing in common with those which I had learned from the captain and which I knew so well! To cut things short, there had been no mistake. It was really a Persian book. I then hoped that the captain, although having forgotten the characters, had nevertheless taught me the language, even perhaps with an imaginary orthography: but this hope was also frustrated. I've turned the world upside down, I've leafed through Persian grammars and anthologies, and in the end, in the end. . ." At this point a sob interrupted poor Y's discourse. "In the end the terrible reality was revealed to me in all its horror: *the captain had not taught me Persian!* No point in telling you with what great anxiety I tried to discover whether his language might be something else—Jakuto, or Hainanese or Hottentot. I got in touch with the most famous linguists in Europe. Nothing, nothing: *such a language did not exist and never had existed!* In my desperation I even wrote to the confounded captain—who had given me his address for whatever he might be able to do for me—and this is the reply which I received from him last night." Y bent his grief-shattered head and handed me a crumpled sheet on which I read:

"Dear Sir: I am in receipt of your letter of. . . etc. A language such as the one you refer to I have never heard mention of, despite my considerable linguistic knowledge." (*The nerve of him!* Y commented.) "The expressions which you quote are absolutely unknown to me and seem, believe me, the product of your fervid imagination. As for the bizarre signs which you have noted down, they resemble on the one hand Aramaic, on the other Tibetan characters, though you may rest assured that they are neither the one nor the other. Concerning the episode of our pleasant relationship, to which you allude, I must answer you sincerely: it is possible that, in teaching you Persian, after so much time I might not have remembered well certain rules or certain words, but I do not see in this any reason for alarm and you will certainly have no trouble in rectifying whatever incorrect notions I may possibly have conveyed to you. I look forward to hearing more good news from you. . . etc."

"Now all is clear," said Y, gaining hold of himself. "I refuse to imagine that the miserable man just wanted to play a trick on me. I believe, rather, that what he taught me he himself considered to be real Persian. His personal Persian, so to speak—an idiom so crippled and defaced as to have nothing in common with the language that inspired it. I reasoned that, in the splendid mind of that pitiful being, his distorted knowledge did not represent a series of stable values, but amidst the fluctuations of his fugitive notions and perhaps under the illusion of reassembling what he had once known, the wretched man had gradually invented the horrible idiom which he taught me; and, as so often happens to this sort of improviser, afterwards he had utterly forgotten his inventions and was sincerely amazed by them."

This diagnosis was pronounced with perfect detachment. But immediately after, Y cried: "He has utterly forgotten them —keep this fact in mind, too! You wanted the facts, well, there they are!" Y shouted as a summing up, momentarily directing his vexation against me. "The saddest part," he said, in a wail, "is that this accursed language, for which I have no name, is very, very beautiful. . .and I love it deeply."

Only when I saw that he had grown calmer did I feel the moment had come for me to speak up.

"Now let's look this over, Y," I began. "What has happened to you is certainly disagreeable. But after all, apart from the wasted effort, is it so serious?"

"That's precisely how people like you think," Y retorted bitterly. "But don't you understand what is serious, what is the dreadful part of this affair? Haven't you understood what is at issue here? What about my three poems? Three poems," he added with great emotion, "into which I poured the best that is in me! My three poems—what kind of poetry are they then? Written in a nonexistent language, it's as if they had not been written in any language! Now come, tell me, what about my three poems?"

All at once I understood what was at stake and in a flash I realized the gravity of the situation. Shaking my head, I admitted: "It is a frightfully original esthetic problem."

"Esthetic·problem, did you say? Esthetic problem. . . well. . . ."

Those were the good old days. We used to get together at night to read the great poets, and a poem had inestimably more importance for us than our bill at the *trattoria,* which continually increased and was never completely paid up.

The next day Y and I knocked at the door of a local publisher, where we were to have a meeting with a great critic, one of those men for whom esthetics hold no secrets and on whose shoulders peacefully rests the spiritual life of an entire nation, since they know the postulates and problems better than anyone else. It had been far from easy to arrange an appointment with such a man, but Y rested his hopes for inner health on this encounter.

The great critic rose to greet us, smiling politely. He was still young and about his lively eyes he had a constant ironic wrinkle. As he spoke, he played now with a steel paper knife, now with a hand-bound book which he twirled along its edge on the desk; often he sniffed the glue which, in its tarnished container, gave off an odor of bitter almonds and, oftener yet, he traced great slashes in the air with long and glittering editorial scissors or used them to smooth down his mustaches. He smiled with restraint, as if to himself, especially when he felt that his interlocutor believed he had caused him some embarrassment. But when he spoke directly to one of us, his smile was worldly and in everything he affected an exaggerated courtesy. He spoke softly, using sober gestures and polished words, duly interspersed with foreign expressions.

Having been apprised of the matter at hand, he seemed to remain for an instant perplexed, then smiled to himself and looking distractedly at a point above our heads, he said:[1]

"But, my dear gentlemen, to write in one language rather than another is perfectly unimportant." (At *portant* he lowered his eyes and emitted a worldly smile.) "It is not necessary that a

[1] I feel it necessary to state that it was the great critic who chose, in addressing us, the second person plural; we followed suit docilely. This circumstance conferred on our colloquy, as the reader will note, a delightfully fantastic tone.

language be very widespread for one to be able to write, let us say, masterpieces in it. This language of yours, Signor Y, is a language spoken by only two persons: that's all. *N'empêche* that your poems can be, ahem, first-rate."

"One moment," said Y. "Didn't I tell you that the English captain has completely forgotten his improvisation of two years ago? What's more, I must confess to you that, seeing the turn taken by the whole affair, I myself burned all my old notes which could have been used to form the grammar or code of the language. So it must therefore be regarded as nonexistent, even for the only two people who spoke it for a few months."

"I hope that you do not believe," the great critic replied, "that the attributes of reality of any language cannot be identified outside of the grammar, the syntax, and I'd even go so far as to say, outside the lexicon. You should simply regard your language as a dead language, capable of being reconstructed only on the basis of some documents which have outlived it—in this case, your three poems—and then the so-called problem is solved. As you know," he added in a conciliating tone, "of some languages we possess only a few inscriptions and thus a very small number of letters, and yet these languages have a great reality. I will say even more: even the languages which are only attested to by the existence of indecipherable, I repeat in-de-ci-pher-able inscriptions, even these languages have a right to our esthetic respect." And, pleased with his sentence, he fell silent.

"But, my dear sir," I then intervened, "leaving aside the languages you have just mentioned—about which I don't believe I have really grasped your idea—and simply dealing with those you mentioned first. . .those languages, I would say, are real inasmuch as their existence is presupposed on the basis of inscriptions, even though meager—but, beware!—presupposed in their lexical, grammatical and syntactical entirety. The inscriptions preserve the traces of a structure, of an articulation which places them in time and space, without which it would be impossible to distinguish them from just any sign marked on just any stone, precisely like the indecipherable languages. These inscriptions, I would say, cast light on an unknown past, yet from that past they gain their very significance. That past is nothing but a complex of norms and conventions which attribute a specific meaning to a specific expression. Now what past can you attribute to my friend's three poems, and from what can they take their meaning? Behind them lies not a complex of norms and conventions, but simply a momentary whim, a whim which has not been codified in any manner and which has vanished as irremediably as it arose."

The great critic looked at me, frowning, still thinking of that "beware" which had annoyed him. Not at all intimidated, I continued:

"A language reconstructed on the basis of meager inscriptions does not acquire substance until one proves that, on the basis of those inscriptions, that language and only that language could be reconstructed. But in our case, on the basis of so fragile a collection of data, it might be possible to construct or reconstruct not one but a hundred languages. Thus one would be confronted by the amusing case of a piece of poetry which could have been written in any one of a hundred languages, each dissimilar from the others and from the first. . . ."

And at this point I stopped talking, rather satisfied with my sophism. But the great critic replied:

"This," he said, "seems to me nothing but a sophism. In the first place, in such cases philology proceeds precisely by suppositions. Suppositions, it is true, which have all the characteristics of relative certainties, but are nevertheless suppositions; nor, theoretically, is just one language reconstructible on the basis of certain inscriptions. In the second place, what does it matter to you that a poem might turn out to be written in more than one language at the same time? The essential is that it be written in one language, and it is beside the point that this language has something in common with another, or, as you say, with a hundred others, so as to permit interchanges of the sort you are imagining. And lastly, I should like to bring it to your attention, my dear sir, from a more, ahem, elevated point of view, that a work of art can be free not only from linguistic conventions but from all conventions and that it creates its own rules."

"Certainly not," I cried, seeing the better part of my argument slipping away. "You can't get out of it that easily. Now you're in danger of relying on a sophism yourself. You are taking it for granted that what is involved is a work of art. But this is precisely what has to be examined: where and what are the criteria you use for your evaluation? Let me sum up my preceding argument. When I said that an inscription has behind it and implies a complex of norms, I meant also that certain of its purely linguistic data are enforced and supported by a knowledge which is not exclusively linguistic: I refer to ethnic knowledge. On the basis of what we know about a certain people, we may even take it for granted that a certain expression is not only valid in one particular position, but also in all other analogous positions. For example, simply knowing that a people has used a given language for its internal and external relationships, provides us with sufficient guarantee of the constant value of a word. Behind an inscription, my dear sir, there is also an entire people! But behind any of these poems there is nothing but a whim. So then, who will guarantee for us that the same expression does not change its meaning radically from one instance to the next? In the separate compositions, or in the very same composition there is, I beg you to observe, not one word which is repeated twice throughout all three poems. Theoretically, my dear sir, one can suppose that each of the three poems unfolds a particular image—or concept, if you prefer—and, at the same time, since not one of the words has a well-defined meaning, one hundred, one thousand, a million other images, or concepts."

"I beg your pardon, I beg your pardon," the great critic shouted, beside himself, "it is just because of this that the problem is quickly resolved. The inscriptions, that is, the poems, can be considered bilingual. Signor Y can always tell us what he intended to say and translate them for us. As you see, your objections do not hold water." And he looked at me triumphantly. But I did not retreat:

"You forget, my dear sir, that a poem is not only an image, or concept, but is constituted of an image, or concept, plus something else. By judging my friend's poems on the basis of the translation which he makes of them, you will find yourself in the position of someone who judges a foreign poet by versions of his work. You must agree that this is neither honest nor honorable.

Furthermore, my friend himself is, strictly speaking, in no position to know what he wanted to say" (Here Y threw me a nasty look.) "since he has conceived his compositions directly in this special language. It follows that his would only be a version, comparable to the one you or I could make, if the need arose, and therefore incomplete and faulty by its very nature. It might even be completely arbitrary and have nothing in common with the text; it could be a false interpretation. Finally, I do not need to remind you, my dear sir, that a work of art is of necessity a realization closely related to certain conventions and judgeable in their light. By its very nature, a result can be evaluated only in terms of the means employed. Except with God, absolute results do not exist, and the very concept of a result is a relative concept. Results range along an infinite ideal scale, though inside the limits of a single moral value. But let us not digress. Well now, my dear sir, what are the criteria you intend to apply to your evaluation?"

A tomblike silence had fallen in the office of the great critic. Letting his eyes stare into the void, he pretended not to have heard my question. He made a show of shaking off a mood of deep contemplation and, to gain time, said to Y, with his most beautiful smile:

"But why, sir, don't you let us hear these famous poems of yours, which are giving rise to such a graceful battle of wits?"

"I have only one poem with me," faltered Y. Encouraged by a sign from the great critic, he drew from his pocket some sheets of paper covered with bizarre and miniscule characters, all slashes and commas, and read in a trembling voice:

> Aga magéra difura natun gua mesciún
> Sánit guggérnis soe-wáli trussán garigúr
> Gúnga bandúra kuttavol jerís-ni gillára.
> Lávi girréscen suttérer lunabinitúr
> Guesc ittanóben katír ma ernáuba gadún
> Vára jesckílla sittáranar gund misagúr,
> Táher chibíll garanóbeven líxta mahára
> Gaj musasciár guen divrés kôes jenabinitúr
> Sðe guadrapútmijen lðeb sierrakár masasciúsc
> Sámm-jab dovár-jab miguélcia gassúta mihúsc
> Sciú munu lússut junáscru garulka varúsc.[2]

In the deep silence which followed, the great critic smoothed his mustaches with the point of the scissors, waiting, while Y bent forward and stared at him. At last Y burst out:

"Did you hear those *u's* in the last lines, did you hear those rhymes in *usc*? Well, what do you think of them?" The poor fellow had forgotten that he owed us some explanation.

"Indeed, indeed, *pas mal,* really *pas mal,*" the great critic said. "Now would you be so kind as to translate?"

Then Y, improvising on the text, translated as follows:

Her weary face crying with happiness,
the woman told me of her life
and assured me of her fraternal affection.
And the pines and larches of the avenue gracefully arched
against the background of the warm-pink sunset
and of a small villa which flew the national flag,

[2]According to the transcription which I later obtained from Y.

seemed the furrowed face of a woman who did not realize
that her nose was shiny. And that shininess flashed
for me a long time, ironic and stinging,
I felt it leap and twist like a little clowning fish
In the shadowy depths of my soul.

"Good, truly very good." The great critic was profuse in
his praise. "Now I understand the reason for all those *u's* in the
last verses! Excellent, excellent. It fits the subject perfectly and
happily it is not at all contrived."

Having taken care of these formalities, he turned to me:

"As you see, your suspicions are unfounded and" (He
smiled.) "rash. Did you notice how fluently he translated?"

"By no means," Y complained. "Such a free translation
does not give the faintest notion of the original. Translated, the
poem is unrecognizable and loses everything. It has been stripped
of all meaning."

"As you see," I said in my turn, "this sets the problem
before us unchanged. A little while ago, my dear sir, I took the
liberty of asking you what criteria you would use. I should now
like to repeat that question."

There was no longer a way out for the great critic, and he
had to consent to reopening the discussion. This he did by again
skirting the difficulty.

"Actually," he began, "I, as you have rightly pointed out,
am not competent to judge these poems; therefore I'm not even
trying to define what criteria should be adopted. The only one
who is competent to judge them is the author himself, just as he
is the only one who knows, more or less, the language."

"If I am not mistaken," I broke in, "I had already implicitly anticipated this statement. Not even the author, since, as I have already said. . ."

But Y, who had remained silent (though I had the impression that he was preparing something), decided to look at it from another angle:

"Do you mean to say that a poem can be a work of art even if there is only one person in the world, only its author, competent to judge it?"

"Precisely."

"Does this mean that from now on in writing poetry one can start with the sound instead of the sense?" These were Y's words, and one had to commiserate with him. "Put together beautiful and sonorous, or evocative and obscure words, and then attribute a meaning to them—or simply see what has come out?"

"Excuse me, I don't quite understand the connection. . ."

"But there is one. Nobody can prevent the poet from arranging the first sounds which flash through his ear according to a particular rhythm, and then attributing to them a beautiful significance. In this way he will create a new language; and little does it matter that this language is truncated and confined to a few sentences—those of the composition—since there will always be someone who knows it, its own creator, and there will always be someone competent to judge the composition: its own author."

"Now, wait a moment, don't go to extremes. Although, if you'll pardon me, it doesn't seem to me very much to the point, I am in full agreement with at least the first part of your argument. But as to the second part, now, please. . .do not *emballer* yourself in a dangerous *Weltanschauung,* do not raise such risky topics. I, personally, prefer commonplaces." The great critic had outdone himself.

But Y replied:

"I don't care, if you'll forgive me, that my argument does not seem to the point. I'm now concerned with determining something else. But you say that you are in agreement with the first part?"

"Of course," the great critic declaimed, "on what takes place in the most secret penetralia of an artist's soul, our profane eyes must not intrude. Of course, an artist is free to put together his words even before attributing a meaning to them, free even to expect from those words, or from a single word, the whole significance and meaning of his composition. Provided that this composition is. . .art. That is what matters. On the other hand, I wouldn't want you to forget that significance and meaning are not at all indispensable. A poem, gentlemen, can also not have meaning. It must only, I repeat, be a work of art."

"Therefore," Y insisted, "a work of art can also not have a common meaning; it can be made up of musical impressions alone and suggest to a hundred million readers a hundred million different things. It can be completely devoid of meaning?"

"That is so, a thousand times, my dear sir."

"Then why the devil do you refuse to admit that even if those sounds are taken from a nonexistent language, what results from it has just as much right to the title of a work of art?"

The great critic glanced furtively at his watch and, thinking perhaps that this interview had already lasted long enough, declared:

"Very well, if you really feel strongly about it, I'll admit it."

"By God, now you're talking!" Y said, smiling. But it seemed to me that his smile had a diabolical nuance. Then he added, with sudden theatrical effect:

"Very well, I renounce the meaning of these poems and I shall bring all of them to you, written out carefully with a facing transliteration so that you can judge them without taking their meaning into account."

"Certainly, certainly," stammered the great critic, taken by surprise, "no doubt, but. . .after all, why do you want to give up their meaning? Why, just think, if you weren't to do so, the path to fame would be much easier, since you would have to reckon with only one person capable of judging you, of appreciating and praising you—that is, with yourself. Believe me, it is better to deal with one person than with too many. Believe me. . .do not be afraid of what might happen if you should, as I hope, come to regard yourself as a great poet, since your fame would be just as complete and full, not even inferior to that of Shakespeare. You would be famous for all those who understand your poetic language, who, by chance, would be one person only. But that hardly counts: fame is not a matter of quantity but of quality. . . ."

The great critic was joking subtly but I could sense that he was in a cold sweat.

"Well then, I surrender to your arguments," Y said at last, and again I saw him sneer to himself. "But you must assure me that on that first point you are completely in agreement with me. You are, aren't you?"

"Of course, of course. Good heavens, absolutely!" The great critic looked at his watch, openly this time, stood up and said:

"Unfortunately my office duties demand my presence elsewhere. Now, to come to a conclusion on the problem which led you to visit me I will say that in the course of our interview we have determined that, for the three poems in question, the only competent judge is their own author, Signor Y, whom I wholeheartedly wish will be able to enjoy in tranquillity his unchallenged fame, which is besmirched by neither envy nor malevolence."

Now that the danger had passed he had reacquired all his assurance. Escorting us to the door, he slapped us familiarly on the shoulders.

"But you won't mind if I come to see you once in a while?" Y asked him.

"Of course, certainly, any time you wish."

I was not at all satisfied and before leaving I tried again:

"But art. . ."

"Art," the great critic broke in, with amiable impatience, "what art is everybody knows."

The sequel to this story is too sad for me to recount it in detail. For the reader it should suffice to know that, after our vist, my friend's brain became slightly addled. A good deal of time has passed, yet he still insists on carrying around from editor to editor strange poems without head or tail, demanding that they be published and that he be paid for them. By now everyone knows him and he is unceremoniously shown the door.

He has stopped going to see the great critic, since the day that, to escape his pestering, that personage himself was compelled to throw him down the stairs. Or something of the sort.

Translated by Raymond Rosenthal

The Two Old Maids

IN A disheartening quarter of a city which itself was in many respects disheartening, on the second floor of a middle-class apartment house, lived two old maids together with their old mother. And the reader can be thankful that I do not feel obliged —as it would appear, other writers so imperiously do—to describe such places in minute detail! If I did, even the best disposed among you would die of melancholy. And I don't see what would be gained by that. So I shall try to confine myself to the bare essentials, which are far too much.

The quarter resounded with the great patriotic battles of the Risorgimento, such as Montebello, Castelfidardo, etc., and the streets thus named ran into or nearby a piazza which was dubbed, needless to say, Piazza Independenza. Yet here all this glory was utterly out of place, even jarring, though it did not in the least disturb the tranquil, worthy and rather somnolent life of both men and things. In short, along those streets, infrequently traversed by vehicles and even pedestrians, between one house and the next extended long tracts of garden wall over which appeared, at intervals, a miserly, dust-laden tree tuft, most likely a eucalyptus or some such vegetable eunuch. These gardens belonged in fact to the many monasteries and convents of the quarter and, since they adjoined the houses, and for other, profounder reasons, spread their domination and odor partly over and within them. Thus, to put everything in one hasty sentence, the air of the entire quarter was saturated with an indefinable miasma of meanness and reaction, in open conflict with its topographical nomenclature. One also caught the whiff of a somewhat hypocritical reserve and, much more pertinently, a smell of votive candles and dirty linen. Not that this very much troubled the righteous composure of the inhabitants; yet to the uninitiated visitor this quarter would always seem a place where most of the people were in partial mourning and forever had sweaty noses. In a word, he would get the sensation that on everything lay an impalpable layer of thin gray dust.

Even the people's talk, a sort of elusive suburban dialect, was soft and unctuous: the jests of the shopkeepers would often go to the borders of scatology—the favorite stamping ground of persons in ecclesiastical garb—but never reached open obscenity. As for so-called modern life, it appeared here in bland, extremely family-like, not to say, bigoted forms. The local movie house, one of those which are called, for good reason, neighborhood houses, almost never had to post the sign: "Minors not admitted." During the intermissions the brats and a few older rowdies would, it's true, amuse themselves by pestering some isolated spectator, shouting across the half-empty hall.

He was, of course, a little old, bald man, with a red face and a stentorian voice. When, however, this party, turning around half astonished and offended, reproached them, indignantly addressing the folded seats: "All the scum of Via Calatafimi, look at them!"—the rowdies simply replied, in a conciliating tone: "These old guys are trying to pick a fight with us!"—and that's where it ended.

The two old maids, whom we shall call Lilla and Nena (diminutives frequent among people of their class), lived in a small second-floor apartment formed of a certain number of cramped rooms, half of which looked on the street and half on a squalid courtyard, the kind where kitchen rags are hung out to dry, carpets are beaten, etc., and from which at all hours of the day rises the most dreary smell of dishwater. But this courtyard was open on one side, separated by a wire fence from one of the convent gardens we've mentioned above. In which garden was placed, one of its walls abutting on the main building, a small chapel that looked like a pavilion and was the convent's church. Sure enough, it was shaded by two eucalyptus trees, whitish and shiny, and the garden, enclosed on its three remaining sides by high walls, could not boast of any other trees or vegetation. It was indeed a melancholy garden, which looked more like a prison yard; at set times one could see the nuns walk through it in silent files to the chapel, or come out, or linger there dazedly for a while.

Such was the habitual view of the two old maids who, because of the kitchen's location in the apartment and the obscurity of the rooms on the street, generally stayed in this part of the house. The apartment itself was furnished in a certain

average and mouldily respectable style, like so many of its kind:
in the parlor, wicker furniture and poker-work pillows; in the
good living room (almost always closed), sofas and armchairs
covered with green velvet and, from the same material, a table
runner trimmed by a ribbon adorned with dainty pink flowers.
For these women were almost rich, though quite stingy, coming
from a small town at the farthest borders of the province, where
they owned land.

Lilla and Nena were both close to sixty. Lilla, thin and
lanky, had a sweeter, more naïve, not to say insipid, character,
suffered from stomach trouble and her nerves, wore a gold pince-
nez tied to one ear by a thin chain of the same metal and also
used a lorgnette which she wore around her neck, a lorgnette one
of whose lenses had been cracked many years before. Nena had
heart trouble, but all in all was much better preserved than her
sister, and this had its effect on her temperament. Both of them
were always dressed in black or, at any rate, in dark clothes,
wearing short dusters or straight, waistless tunics, their shoulders
covered by short tippets of purple wool or gray woolen shawls;
their hair, often disheveled and standing out spikily at the neck
and temples, was also grayish and vaguely red, due to certain
old-fashioned efforts to keep it black; and finally, on their faces,
in the furrows between the nostrils and the cheeks, and in some
of the deeper wrinkles, perennially stagnated a thick sweat, like
tallow.

Their life had been and was now, except for what we are
about to relate, pretty much what one might imagine, and there's
no need to waste too many words on it. The circle of their

relatives included distant or very distant kin (since they no longer had any close ones) and suchlike, whose visits they received every so often, although rarely did they return them. Among these it may be in place to mention briefly at least the head clerk at the Ministry of Agriculture, a man with very bulging eyes and bad breath, who had, despite certain literary yearnings in his youth, yellowed at his desk. A man of great outward and verbal vehemence, who made a big point (as he often insisted) of calling a spade a spade, and did not hesitate to describe his office as "the most filthy glob of spit in the ministerial cuspidor," with which dubious ambiguity he certainly intended to cast discredit on his entire ministry.

A Rear Admiral, yellow too, with half his head husked of its hair, a long nose but almost no chin; who, when he talked, dropped words from that very hairy nose, like bits of snot (a manner of talking which some boys call "snot-snuffling," a hypotyposis which these little impudents also use in regard to another function somewhat less important than speech). Rear Admiral speaks to the heart of generous exploits, vast, free spaces and far-off lands. But, alas, this man had not sailed except in his distant youth, then only to become an ensign, and he too had spent the remainder of his career in the office of a ministry; and now he was a God-fearing officer, who only insisted that his sons, gangly adolescents, wear blue sailor sweaters, no matter what the season.

An old, bemustached spinster with an unexpected first name, who "knew German better than Italian," nor was there any other way of identifying her. From her quacky voice the old maids had been forced to learn some brief phrases in that language, such as "Wie geht's Ihnen?"; "Ja, und?; ach, wo!" and a few others less correct.

And other people of the same sort. To which one might add, beyond the immediate circle of relatives, a few particularly respectable fellow-tenants. For example, the Senator on the third floor, an old, senile man, once Undersecretary of Public Works, who, however, had never set foot in the old maids' apartment, being content to receive their visits a few times a year; some occasional acquaintances; and then the seamstress, one or two shopkeepers and a rather large number of nuns, monks, priests, deacons and such folk, who came not only for contributions but also to pass the time. Certainly there's no need to mention that the two old maids were extremely devout, though each according to her own bent.

Whenever one of these squalid personages appeared at the door of their apartment, the two sisters, having quickly come into the dark entrance hall, would welcome them with reiterated nods of the head and liftings of the arms, every time as though they hadn't seen him or her for at least ten years, and then go on welcoming the visitor, each in her special fashion—Lilla, emitting certain self-confident grunts, the other sister quavery "ohs" and "ahs." Afterwards, depending on the visitor, they would go into the parlor or the good living room (or even more often, as we shall see, into their old mother's bedroom). Here they all sat down with their hands on their knees and here was served the coffee, duly blended with barley from their holdings in the country. And then the conversation began, with its inevitable accompaniment of "You don't say!" "Oh, really?"

and "Oh, God help us!" and, now and then, the sign of the cross executed by the ladies of the house. For the guests always had something scandalous to recount, something which pious, respectable people cannot hear without quaking indignantly and which demanded on the part of the narrator, especially if a woman, a final, emphatic "Did you ever hear such a thing!" which more or less meant: "So you see what a pass we've come to and in what calamitous times we live!" Or the conversation would deal with the affairs and doings of their fellow townsmen, whose slightest acts and aims, as with everything that happened in the town, the old maids always managed to hear about even before, and in greater detail, the very persons involved did. And then, if the visitor was one of their intimates and the time for the afternoon snack had come, there appeared the specialty called "dainty egg," originating no doubt in some nun's school—that is, an omelet with one or more large slices of bread folded into it, so that the egg was nothing more than a very thin layer over the bread, and perhaps one egg was enough to make two "dainty eggs."

But certainly the reader has by now a pretty clear notion of the scene and gladly dispenses me from adding other touches to this faithful picture.

2

As we've said, the two old maids lived with their old mother; and, we might add, a rather elderly maid, who was wholly wedded to their cause and had, without realizing it, patterned herself after them. It goes without saying that this person, though without the least forwardness and never, or almost never, to her own advantage, lorded it in the house, and her opinion was highly prized in every emergency. As for the mother, the decrepit as well as aged Signora Marietta was a notable example of her species (although not so rare as it might seem), therefore we feel that we ought to devote a few words to her.

She was, of course, sick; but what her sickness was no bearded specialist had ever been able to determine. Nervous and authoritarian she had always been; however, around her seventieth or seventy-fifth year the expressions of this predisposition had grown more and more alarming, until they became real symptoms, varying only in magnitude. One fine day the old lady began to complain of vague pains at several, unspecifiable points in her body, and after a year she was replying to the visitors who inquired about her health: "How are you, Donna Marietta?"— with the laconic singsong which the old maids never stopped hearing for some ten years and more: "Terrible pains." After another two or three years she had adopted the other, more constant singsong, which did not need to be elicited and would suddenly explode in the silence or right in the middle of a discourse of a much different tenor: "What pains! What pains! Oh, oh, I can't stand it any more."

This sentence was always pronounced in the same, strangely musical tone: the first four words were high-pitched, like an enraged, shrilling blast, and the remainder gradually petered out in a kind of triumphant despair. The old woman was most likely fond of her illness, since it permitted her to continue to exercise her power over her daughters and throughout the house; indeed, one might suspect that, feeling her strength ebbing away, she had purposely clutched the only weapon left to keep the people around her in subjection—she had purposely fallen ill. For no organic fault had ever been discovered, and her pains, which no sedative could relieve, continued to be unlocatable and elusive. But the illness, whether natural or willed, dragged her little by little to the grave, nor was her good appetite, which never failed her right down to the last day, of any avail. At first she had to spend the greater part of the day in an armchair; toward the end she could no longer leave her bed, where she was struck, during the last years, by a stiffening of her legs and almost her entire body, though she could still move her arms, or rather her forearms. At that point she stopped talking, though she still made herself very well understood.

The outward manifestations of the disease, whose true nature remained hidden from all, consisted predominantly in frenzies of various kinds and differing intensities; these rages, unfailingly increased beyond all bounds if the old maids so much as left the sick woman's bedside, or even as soon as they showed the slightest intention of doing so. The old woman was endowed with more than animal sensitivity and could read the thoughts of her victims. If Lilla (who, being delicate, should have been out in the fresh air as much as possible) were preparing, even in a room far from her mother's, to slip out secretly for a half hour, the old woman would start screaming as loud and long as she could. She would beat her sides or punch herself on the head—in short, raise the very devil. The most trivial things could bring on this intemperateness: for instance, if one of the old maids had to go "to Paris"—another expression from some nun's school, as everyone can see. No matter what it was that didn't suit her, the old woman would begin to maltreat herself, thereby giving further proof of her insight; and the old maids and the servant rushed to restrain her and to remove the cause of her agitation. Then, with the passing of the years, the prohibition against leaving the house or leaving her side in any fashion, at first limited to the two old maids, was extended to the servant and finally to the pets, about whom I shall speak further on.

We must not think that Donna Marietta always wanted people around her because she was truly in need of assistance; in fact, if someone left the room even when she was sleeping placidly, she woke up with a jerk and started the usual pantomime. Having gathered all the occupants of the house around her like a mangy hen her chicks, she did nothing but intone: "What pains! What pains! Oh, oh, I can't stand it anymore!" or stare at them in silence, since she almost never had anything definite to ask of them. Poor old woman, that was the only order she could now impose: her own presence. And if you think of it, just those two chicks nearly added up to two centuries! But that's how it goes: mothers never learn to regard their offspring as grown up.

It is easy to imagine the kind of life this determined old lady made for the three other women. Dominated as they had always been by her will, dismayed at seeing even their slightest schemes exposed, the old maids retreated, if not into themselves, at least into their holes, giving up all thought of moving about save in cases of extreme necessity and renouncing all their own personal impulses.

Despite her complaints, Donna Marietta's illness worsened with exceptional slowness. During the years in the armchair she would still sometimes, though infrequently, talk about small matters and even laugh, silently shaking her belly. This was the only sign she gave of enjoying anything. But when she had become bedridden she gave her full attention only to her illness and her obsession. Yet another two or three years passed before she was overtaken by the stiffening of her body. But neither this nor the cessation of speech which accompanied it, overwhelmed her strong constitution before still another three years had gone by.

During the last period she had been reduced to a block of wood, having all the attributes of death save for color and loss of appetite. And yet, gnarled just like an old stump and equally as inert, her eyes half dead and staring, she nevertheless clung to her customary and most personal mode of expression: beating herself. Her forearms were untouched by the paralysis, and she could still beat her chest at the level of her shoulder blades; this beating produced a hollow, lugubrious sound—*tock tock*— more like that of an African kettledrum than the notorious, gay big bass drum. This *tock tock* (two raps were the general rule) eventually assumed the significance of a simple negation, immediately robbing the questioner of any foolish desire to go on asking. For instance: "Donna Marietta, or Mama, would you like some consommé?"—Answer: "*Tock tock*."—"All right, then, I'll bring you your milk."—"*Tock tock*."—"But you've got to eat something." Here the raps became stronger and the interlocutrix, if we may call her that, grasped the old woman's arms. Then: "But say I put some noodles in the consommé?" Absolute immobility, the sign of assent. In fact, right to the last, although her head was rigid, the old woman continued not only to eat but also to masticate.

Since they always fussed over her and she almost always answered "no," this *tock tock* had become the house's true voice. Nevertheless one day she faded out, for, in the end, even such a mother eventually manages to die. Lilla had gotten up to leave the room, but no *tock tock* resounded to detain her—it became quite clear that the old woman was dead. Her head by now was nothing but a skull. A skull—and here follows a detail which, though belated, I consider very apposite—bearded and mustachioed beyond all reasonable imagining and in a completely masculine fashion, as Donna Marietta's head had always been.

Over this skull, crazed by the presence of the corpse and plummeting down from the top of the closet, there came for a moment to bend its deformed face with heart-rending whimpers—the monkey. This monkey, who only now enters on the scene for the first time, is actually the true protagonist, indeed the hero of this story. Donna Marietta has no real role in it, since she has, it seems, renounced that of a ghost, which such characters more often than not will play after death. I have dwelt on her simply out of a love of completeness; and the very same scruple now demands that, before going on and getting to the heart of my story, I briefly mention a small bird which was also a member of the household.

It was, needless to say, a "cardinal bird," so named because of its crest or little cap of a sodden and funereal red. It was about the size of a shrike, or a little bit larger, and had a calm and resigned character; usually it lived in a cage hanging on a balcony overlooking the courtyard, until the old woman insisted on having it in her room, where the unhappy bird languished miserably (the room was never aired). The old maids were very fond of it and fed it chiefly on moistened sponge cake. But the full tide of their affections was reserved for someone else; and so, at this point, we must leave this bird to its obscurity.

3

The monkey was a rather small, vivacious animal, probably a Cercopithecus; but it will be best to give up from the start any attempt to describe him in detail and as a distinct entity—which, I can wager, will be greeted with great relief by the reader. For, in truth, all the qualities that an alert storyteller of the human species, expert as he may be in probing character, can notice in, or attribute to, an animal, are after all but mere suppositions to which only our immoderate anthropomorphism lends verisimilitude. Just between ourselves: How can anyone penetrate the thoughts of a brute, the true meaning of his acts, even if we adopt the human conception of such terms? One man in relation to another possesses, if nothing else, at least a convention of language by which to measure his qualities; but to transfer this convention to animals would be, to say the least, arbitrary. By what standard, for example, may a monkey be judged good or bad? So we might as well confess agnostically and from the very start that we're absolutely in the dark, and close this embarrassing parenthesis. Well then, this monkey was a monkey, with all the external attributes and apparent characteristics of his species; he was a mysterious creature. We should explain, however, so that his presence in the house of the two old maids does not seem extraordinary, that many years before they'd had a brother, who had left home at an early age and become a sea captain (perhaps with the assistance of the now Rear Admiral). This brother, returning from one of his voyages, had brought the monkey to their home town, a monkey which had just been torn from his mother's breast. The brother died soon after on foreign soil and the sisters, who had gradually concentrated on him all the affection of which they were capable—not a little, certainly—and solely to him had dedicated the beats of their feminine hearts, now poured this affection onto the animal. By now he was doubly and trebly dear to them.

It is man's custom to keep the object of his love, if at all possible, caged. And a large cage was the habitual residence of the monkey; for greater security there was a sort of pectoral harness which was locked on his back, and attached to this a small chain whose other end was fastened inside the cage, giving him complete freedom of movement within it. The beast proved to be very restless; nor, though duly castrated and with his teeth filed down, did he seem to lose any of his natural turbulence. He often shrieked or chittered like a child, without a plausible reason; he complained, went into rages over nothing, threatened to leap at the faces of unfamiliar people, sometimes even at his mistresses, and at such times his extraordinarily mobile eyes lit up with terrifying hatred.

"But at bottom he's so good!" the old maids would always say. And indeed it was often enough to give him, as a "diversion," a walnut, which he cracked between his molars and diligently picked apart and ate with great concentration. When let out of the cage, he behaved much more reasonably—which is no cause for wonder; the old maids had therefore taken to giving him his freedom occasionally, of course, in a closed room. There he was free to climb on the furniture, which he did with great delicacy and without ever breaking anything, poking about to his heart's content; and he would stop his unreasonable whimperings. However, even then he did not cease to manifest, by some small aspect of his behavior, a certain bossiness. Though a eunuch, he was after all the male of the house and spoiled to boot, despite the pitiable life he led. When he was free and had let off as much steam as he wished, his tiny eyes began to close like a child's and he sought refuge on the lap of one of the two women, Lilla's, usually; or better, if she was lying down, he would attach himself to her breasts, which he clutched with all four of his extremities in a pose of possession. The monkey began to develop these virile traits especially after the death of Donna Marietta: the bemustached and bearded old lady had filled him with a perplexed and perhaps envious sense of subjugation which bordered on terror. But at this point I realize that I have let myself slip into the above-deprecated misdemeanor, that of attributing human attitudes and feelings to a brute—and therefore I put a full stop.

Though far from being completely liberated from the nightmare which their mother had created for them, the two old maids were at least relieved of her presence and were beginning to enjoy a certain tranquillity, when suddenly the lightning struck. Let us try to recall everything which I have so laboriously set down until now and then draw our conclusions.

One fine morning the Mother Superior of the neighboring convent appeared at their door with a circumspect and mysterious air. The two old maids had a slight acquaintance with her, because they sometimes bestowed their leftovers on the convent's poor. Led into the green drawing room, she said first of all that she knew from experience of their uncrushable faith and the God-fearing, exemplary sobriety of their way of life, which made the information she was about to impart all the more painful for her; finally, after many more preliminaries she explained that she could no longer keep quiet about what was taking place in the convent owing to the activities of an animal that belonged to them. The old maids were utterly astounded and anxiously pressed her for an explanation—which she at last gave.

The nun accused the monkey of having penetrated furtively at night into their chapel beneath the eucalyptus trees, and of having removed or eaten a certain number of consecrated hosts. Furthermore, he had drunk some wine which, if not consecrated, was nevertheless sacred. This sacrilegious theft, or sacrilegious ingestion, was not, she declared, a unique occurrence but had been going on for some time now and, just to cite the most recent incident, had taken place again the night before.

There was, unfortunately, no longer any doubt as to the identity of the perpetrator, for if that had been the case she would not have taken it upon herself to, etc., etc.

Omitting the old maids' "oh's" and "ah's" which were unleashed by this extraordinary affair, I will try as faithfully as possible to adhere to the bare account of the events that followed.

Of the two, Nena was the first to regain control of herself; while Lilla was still pouring forth apologies and, with unconscious blasphemy, offers of compensation, Nena demanded that the nun furnish some explanations and justify her suspicions. Not suspicions, the nun retorted, a trifle put out, but absolute certainty: some of the sisters, struck by the inexplicable loss of the sacred comestibles, had kept vigil, spied, remained on the lookout, till at last, the night before, they had caught sight of a small shadow which. . .and besides, for the past few months they had often seen the monkey—in its cage, that's true—on the balcony overlooking the nunnery's garden or next to the kitchen window, which faced in the same direction; and he seemed to be following with interest the movements of the nuns, and. . . .

"My goodness, all the things you've observed, my dear Mother Superior!" Nena broke in. "But beware of rash suspicions," she added, smiling. "I'll admit that our Tombo (which, originally spelled Tomboo, was the monkey's name) is a bit unruly, but he'd never do a thing like that. Please be kind enough to come with me."

And she led the Mother Superior straight into the kitchen. Nena was trying very hard to keep her temper, but she was deeply troubled and insulted, as though her honor were at stake if the monkey should prove to be guilty. The party in question, locked and tethered in his prison, was busy picking his fleas under a weak beam of sunlight which fell obliquely through the open window; when he saw the stranger, he threatened to pounce on her, as he usually did, but then immediately calmed down and set himself to observe with great attention this black personage surmounted by so enthralling a headdress.

"Just look, Mother," Nena continued, pointing at the cage. "Certainly we didn't let him out, and how could he have freed himself, I'd like to know? See for yourself if such a little beast could snap a chain like this and break down this kind of door! Anyway, the chain would be broken, isn't that so? And what about the door, isn't it locked from outside? Nothing's been touched. . . . No, no, my dear Mother, there's definitely been a mistake here."

"And yet!" the Mother Superior insisted.

Just then a file of nuns began to cross the convent garden below, heading slowly for the chapel, the site of the presumed crime. The monkey who, bored with examining the Mother Superior, had turned to the window, on seeing the nuns gave signs of the liveliest interest; he cocked his head to one side, clutched the bars, hopped up and down, holding his feet together and slapping his knees, and frowned—and made other brusque and grotesque little gestures. He appeared to be greatly amused.

"There! You see what I mean?" the Mother Superior cried.

"But what's that got to do with it, he always acts like this," Lilla asserted incautiously.

"That's just it!" the Mother Superior remarked mysteriously.

The nuns had disappeared.

"No, no," Nena repeated peremptorily, in order to end the matter. "There's no doubt you've made a mistake."

Given these terms, the discussion could not proceed any further. The Mother Superior, in view of Nena's resistance, changed her tone somewhat and assumed an air of unctuous commiseration, as though she sincerely pitied the old maids for having such a rascal in their house; she advised them to keep an eye on the animal, since it would be regrettable if in the house of Our Lord, etc., and the two women gladly promised to do just that. Then, though not without having accepted some small alms for the poor of the quarter, she withdrew, rather perplexed: she could only up to a certain point understand Nena's obstinate desire to clear her monkey of all guilt.

After the nun had left, Nena's attitude suddenly changed and her assurance became a kind of anxious dismay. She began pacing through the rooms, wringing her hands, and repeating: "Could it be possible? And yet. . .but how could he have done it?"—and similar phrases. Lilla, whom Nena's attitude had to some extent roused from the foolish consternation which at first had gripped her, now succumbed to it again; and both of them, together with the maid, who'd been quickly involved, began chattering frantically about this unbelievable affair. Nena did not really give too much credence to the possibility of such a deed on the part of the monkey, but just the thought that someone might even suspect their Tombo deeply humiliated her. The other two women had each her own opinion. The arguments, the conjectures, the advice given and received—while the three of them worked each other up, calmed each other down, and persuaded each other—lasted all that day and the next too, not to mention a good part of the nights. Also some of their visitors were informed of the affair, though under a vow of secrecy, and no doubt each of them volunteered an opinion on the subject.

Those were two terrible days for the old maids; but even worse were in store for them. Finally it was decided to regard the entire matter as trivial, at least for the time being, and the monkey, at first removed to the bedroom, just to be sure, was carried back to his place in the kitchen, since he stank at night and, furthermore, the storm having subsided somewhat, his innocence had been, so to speak, recognized. But the old maids still had their hearts in their mouths. Then on the morning of the third day, when the hornet's nest was just about to stop buzzing, a wide-eyed nun came with a message from the Mother Superior, saying briefly that the theft of the sacred staples had been repeated that very night and that the monkey had nearly been caught in the act; and immediately she left without another word.

I omit the description of the women's response to this announcement. It was decided to spy on the monkey, beginning that very night. The reasons for this procedure, which Nena demanded, perhaps will not be very clear to everyone. Why, one might ask, didn't the old maids just lock the animal in a room, at least during the night? An exact answer would perhaps be neither easy nor very simple, and I will spare the reader. Let me simply point out here that for Nena it was probably not so much a matter of physically inhibiting the monkey as of making an adequate appraisal of his morality.

"You know," she said gloomily to her sister, at a moment when they were alone in the evening, "you know how much I

love Tombo; but if he really did what they say, I want to put
him into his little coffin with my own hands!"

4

Two or three nights passed before the women, who took
turns watching, were able to surprise the monkey in any serious
infraction of the rules of the house—or, to put it bluntly, in the
flagrant crimes of noctambulism or deviousness. They had agreed
that throughout the night at least one of them would stay awake
and silently take up a position, at the usual bedtime, on an
armchair situated in a bedroom which looked out on the short
hallway leading to the kitchen; through the two doors, which
had been left ajar, the sentinel's eye fell directly on the animal's
cage, which was sufficiently illuminated by the small electric
candle burning day and night in the kitchen before an image
of the Madonna. This night watchman must of course be careful
not to make suspicious noises, so that the monkey would be led
to believe that the ladies of the house were, as always, sound
asleep, and would not notice any irregularity in their habits; and
the sentinel should raise the alarm at the slightest movement
worthy of note.

The first nights the beast slept placidly on his pallet of
woolen rags in a corner of the cage, only waking up every hour
or two to scratch himself furiously or to grumble, so it seemed,
about something. Once or twice he even got up and pottered
about for a quarter of an hour, as though he wanted to stretch

his arms and legs—a restlessness which remained, however, without consequence. On the fourth night, Nena was on guard; she had become more and more convinced that Tombo was innocent and above all suspicion, and now she was almost dozing. When, all of a sudden, she had a blurred vision of the animal who, having as usual stood up, scratched himself, and moved up and down the cage, was now shaking the bars next to the small door with silent fury. This brought her fully awake and made her sharpen her eyes.

Tombo withdrew, but only to indulge in a series of frenetic quakings and contortions, like those of a dog when it tries to shake off water, or those of a cat when it wants to rid itself of some restraint or nuisance, yet whose purpose wasn't too clear— and all this very, very silently. Before Nena could realize what was happening, the beast stood there, freed of his halter as well as his chain. So he had indeed found a way! This was certainly not the first time—the operation seemed to be a familiar one for him. Holding her breath, the old maid watched every move he made.

Tombo again approached the door of the cage and shook it with his particular cautious fury. When he saw that it did not give way, he changed his tactics. It must be mentioned that all around this door ran a band of sheet metal, which had purposely been put there so that the prisoner could not, if it ever came into his head, stretch his hand through the bars and open the door from the outside. However, the maker of the cage had reckoned only approximately with the natural intelligence of the animal it was meant to house. Now the monkey, clinging to the bars which ran alongside and over the metal strip, climbed up far enough to be above the obstacle, and from up there stretched his arm, which proved to be disproportionately long, toward the latch which locked the door from the outside. But even in this way he did not manage to reach it. One might have thought that so far he had simply transferred the difficulty to another place, and yet he had his reasons: he had become convinced that the latch could be maneuvered better from above than from the side. He descended again and now with great decisiveness made for a little trapeze which hung in the cage for his amusement, and skillfully plucked out the horizontal bar, which must already have been loosened. This operation, as well as another similar to it which we shall soon describe, he must surely have seen done before. Equipped with this tool, he returned to his place above the door and, again thrusting out his arm, whose length was now increased by that of the stick, after some fumbling about at last managed to jiggle the latch and make it fall back: the cage was open.

At this juncture Nena wanted to give the alarm, but she could not do so without arousing the monkey's suspicions. Yet Tombo did not seem in a hurry to take advantage of his conquered freedom, almost as though he had done everything for the fun of it or to test his dexterity; so the old maid began to feel hopeful again.

Tombo was now in a corner of the cage near his pallet, where he kept turning around and around with little snorts and puffs, bending his knees a bit, as though he were trying to find the most comfortable position in which to lie down—just as dogs do sometimes. Then he stopped moving and remained for some time motionless, half-seated and with his hands propped against the floor of the cage. At last he got to his feet and stretched, after which he gave a wide yawn, scratching his belly; he also emitted a barely audible chitter. Nena did not miss a single one of these movements and sounds. Now the animal seemed to be making up his mind to do something, and his entire body expressed this determination. He turned to right and left in his usual abrupt manner. His eyes sparkled. He remained immobile for another instant, as though listening, then he hopped toward the door. But he tripped on a tin cup which was there for his water; so he halted, moodily, to get it out of his way, or rather to beat it childishly, as if punishing it for its impudence. Again a long spell of immobility, caused either by distraction or by the fear that the slight fracas had awakened someone. This was followed by a new decision; and this time Tombo pushed at the door of the cage.

The cage was placed on a large, unpainted table. Clutching one of its legs, the monkey descended to the floor, which he crossed two or three times this way and that, seeming not very sure of the direction to take. To Nena, aside from her anguish, it was a shock to see him there on the floor, destined as he was to live aloft; but it wasn't only this. The beast, who, of course, walked with the help of his hands, looked to her somehow unmentionable and disgusting in that dim, nocturnal light—like the Buprestis or the stag beetle when, threatened, they detach themselves from the ground against which they were flattened and, rising high on their long legs, dash away rapidly and furtively. Or, more simply, he resembled a monstrous spider. Now, at last, he definitely decided on his course: having climbed by the same route up onto the table next to the window, grasping first the bars of the cage, then the knob of the window, he lifted himself onto the window sill. (Why he preferred this round-about method to a quick leap, it would be hard to say.) The shutters were pulled to, but not enough to prevent the passage of that tiny body between the sill and the frame. Having for a moment scrutinized the darkness outside and clinging with one hand to a slat, the monkey lowered himself into the gulf, then withdrew his hand, which must have found another grip, and so vanished from the old maid's sight. Rushing silently to the window of a room next to the kitchen, she reached there in time to see him leap to the ground from the end of a rainspout which ran a few feet away from the shutters of the kitchen window. Helped by the air's vague luminosity, she could follow, step by step, his swift yet circumspect gyrations; which led him in a few instants past the wire fence into the garden of the nunnery. But here the animal was engulfed by the shadow of the two eucalyptus trees and Nena inevitably lost sight of him. Nonetheless it seemed to her that he had climbed one of those trees; at any rate, he had not gone toward the chapel. Nena left the window—it can easily be imagined in what a state—and at last gave the alarm.

Being careful not to make any noise and not to turn on any lights on the side facing the courtyard, the three women gathered at the window from which Nena had watched the monkey disappear. The first thought which spontaneously came to all three of them was not to arouse the animal's suspicions even now, so that they could watch his return. They must find out more about Tombo's behavior; if he did not know he'd been discovered, he might furnish precise clues concerning his nocturnal activities. There is no need to add, of course, that for the old maids his little jaunt was not yet sufficient proof of criminal proceedings in the chapel. At least not for Lilla and Apollonia, or "Bellonia" as they called the maid. Nena was so deeply distraught that she could barely think, much less draw any sort of conclusion. To her, the monkey's misconduct in itself appeared overwhelming, whereas the others seemed prepared to regard it rather indulgently, so long as it had no consequences. Nena felt betrayed, abused, and was now forlornly pacing up and down the room, and all that she could say was: "He shouldn't have done this to me!"

Meanwhile Lilla and Bellonia, half undressed, just as they'd jumped out of bed, were keeping an eye on the garden and courtyard, exchanging comments in a whisper; a dim gleam, not enough to make out anything in the room distinctly, came from the window. After a while, Nena's behavior began to worry them. The maid nudged her mistress with her elbow and Lilla went to her sister. For a time she tagged after her in her agitated pacing, without knowing what to say. She would have liked to console her, though she wasn't quite sure what she should console her for, since she did not understand her sorrow. In the end she started to say that perhaps Tombo hadn't gone to the chapel at all, perhaps he only wanted to go out for a while.

"But what has this got to do with it?" Nena retorted sternly, without halting.

Lilla, intimidated, gave vent to a series of mumbles, grunts, and vague little phrases such as "I mean. . .am I right. . .do you realize" and so on, whose general meaning was that after all there was no point in taking it so hard, because animals are only animals.

Nena stopped pacing abruptly and repeated to herself: "Animals!" as if she had just at that moment realized that Tombo was an animal.

More than an hour went by. Finally Bellonia announced in a rapid whisper that the monkey was on his way back. Emerging from the shadow of one of the eucalyptus trees, though at a spot some distance from the chapel, Tombo came hopping, without undue haste, toward the dividing fence. The women dashed away from the window and stationed themselves to watch from the hallway. And from there they witnessed an inverse repetition of the scene described above. He re-entered by the same route, and after dawdling about on the furniture for a while, shut himself in the cage, pulled the door to behind him, and made sure that the latch was back in place, maneuvering it this time from the side. Then, by dint of pitiful and laborious contortions, he managed to slip on the halter again; and there he sat, looking dazed. This particular behavior of his—the fact that he tidied up everything so neatly—seemed definitive proof that these jaunts were habitual, and that he had no intention of giving them up.

From his mood of stupefaction Tombo soon passed to a curious agitation. He capered about wildly, and every so often ran with prodigious speed three or four times around the cage, up and down and from right to left, following an approximately circular orbit—more like a crazed rabbit than a monkey. Yet as soon as Bellonia entered the kitchen for her chores (dawn had come and the good maid could no longer think of going back to bed), he threw himself with a crash on his pallet and pretended to be sleeping. For the time being nobody said a word to him, obeying Nena's orders, who confusedly announced that she wanted to spy on him some more, and so he must not know that he'd been discovered.

Now the old maids retired to get some rest. They had barely closed their eyes when news of a new sacrilege at the chapel arrived. This time, so as not to offend the pious ladies, the nun sent from the convent had simply given the message to the porter who, knowing that the old maids were early risers, had come upstairs right away.

With the result, on top of everything else, that the story began to spread and the whole house, soon the whole quarter, was informed of the ignominious suspicion, now a certainty, which weighed on Tombo. The nuns of the convent did not cut the most flattering figure in this affair. Some people claimed that they had heard violent nocturnal uproars in the convent— presumably because the sisters had at first mistaken Tombo for a devil with a tail who'd come up from hell to punish them for their sins. But then, we all know how vivid the popular imagination is.

5

On the day which followed that agitated night Nena had almost regained control of herself, or at least so it seemed. She repeated her version of what she had seen to her sister and the maid, and together they discussed the problem at length. But as Lilla and Bellonia became more and more convinced of Tombo's responsibility in the desecration of the hosts and, seeing her calmer, forthrightly affirmed it, Nena denied it more and more openly. That the monkey might be the sort to skip out secretly and go to cavort in the eucalyptus trees, she could not, she said, deny; yet quite a distance separated one thing from the other. "Why, of course not!" she concluded each time, as she walked up and down the room, trailing the strings of her bloomers, since that day they hadn't even given a thought to getting properly dressed. "Why, of course not," she repeated, "He's incapable of doing such a thing!"

Nena—to deal with this point once and for all—had one of those temperaments which unconsciously fear themselves, and must at all costs acquire absolute certainty, since they know that matters left in doubt will give rise in them to intimate or open reactions of an irreparable kind. Nor do they prefer to avoid these reactions by keeping themselves in a state of relative ignorance; on the contrary they look for and hope for decisive proof, all the more if it may turn out to be painful to them. Cruel temperaments—or at least close to the point of cruelty. But this is facile psychology, and I do not guarantee the accuracy of the interpretation. Who can say what Nena really and truly thought and felt in this situation? I don't presume to explain anything, and so I return to my story.

"Of course not, of course not," she went on, shaking her head. While her sister was already trying to plan how they could restrain the monkey in the future. "Do you realize, eh, I mean an animal who opens doors, takes off his collar. Am I right? What shall we do?" And then a flood of mumbles and grunts poured out, endlessly. But suddenly it looked as if Nena had thought of something and, without delay, she began to get dressed very correctly, while the other two trailed around after her, asking for an explanation. She curtly declared that she was going to visit the convent next door. "I don't believe it," she said. "I won't believe it until I've seen it with my own eyes!"

She was going to ask the Mother Superior for something which the other women regarded as unheard-of, contrary to all custom, the idea of someone completely unhinged: that is, permission to watch that night in the chapel and, if so it must be, catch the beast red-handed. The other women tried in every way to dissuade her, but she just went straight ahead. Putting on her bird-adorned hat, she said:

"Go and see if he needs anything. Don't ask me to go, I don't want to see him. And if it turns out to be true," she added, as she left, "then we'll think about what we have to do. Right now, there's no point in discussing it any more."

It is not known how Nena managed things with the Mother Superior. The latter certainly must have been astounded, seeing that respectable and devout little old lady so concerned about her monkey's morality, when all she had to do was just chain him a bit more securely. Or, more likely the touchy nun was insulted because the community had not been taken at its word, although, in truth, the only positive thing her flock had glimpsed was a shadow. But this was a delicate business: to offend two rather munificent benefactors wasn't to her best interest, so the Mother Superior ended by lending herself to this folly, in all likelihood after having consulted with her spiritual director and God knows how many other people. The fact remains that Nena came home after an hour, fairly exhausted and with her nose more sweaty than ever, but having obtained what she wanted. Then she kept silent for the remainder of the day, slept for a while, and that very evening prepared for her new vigil.

They had agreed that one of the two who stayed at home would spy on the monkey as before, since Nena, stationed inside the chapel, could not watch all his movements. That night neither of the two lookouts noted anything suspicious: the monkey slept more or less quietly. After having returned home and received the report of her aide, Nena assumed a strange expression of triumph mixed with disappointment, which soon resolved into a reassured tenderness. After the second night this expression, and the mood which followed it, became more intense, for although Tombo had left the cage and the house he had not appeared in the chapel. This was already a long stride on the path to his partial rehabilitation. "Didn't I say so!" Nena murmured. On the third night. . .

Nena was almost never alone during her vigils in the chapel; since the convent, among other things, helped care for the sick, one or another of the sisters on duty kept her company and most likely kept an eye on her, no doubt by order of the Mother Superior. On this third night, her companion was a young and timid nun with a provincial accent, who had perhaps barely donned the habit and became flustered and blushed if one merely looked at her. The two women had taken up the same posts as on the previous nights, that is, in a small sacristy between the chapel and the main building, and whose door they had left slightly ajar. In their field of vision they had, to their right, the outer door of the chapel, which opened on the garden with the two eucalyptus trees and was locked, of course, from the inside; to their left, but actually, right opposite them, the altar, which they saw from the side, more or less as one sees a stage-set from the wings. Since the small lamp which the nuns always kept lit on this altar did not suffice to light up the scene adequately and irrefutably (it was one of those lamps with a floating wick, nearly covered by the oil, which could not dispel the darkness), the old maid had gotten permission to burn, at her own expense, two thick candles at each side of the tabernacle. So the illumination was, one might say, quite festive, considering the smallness of the chapel.

The door of that sacred place was surmounted by a fanlight shaped like a peacock's tail; it had no glass, but rather closely set bars, though not perhaps close enough to stop a monkey from entering. That was the only opening through which the animal could possibly have gained admission, since from that fanlight, if one excepted the door, the chapel received its only light; and in fact, the nuns claimed that they had seen the monkey escape through it several times. So the two women were crouching there quietly in the dark, keeping their eyes fixed on that particular spot. They had both settled down, the guest—one does not know how welcome—on a big, stuffed chair, probably the appurtenance of the bishop or father confessor, the nun on a bench. They were muttering their prayers, interspersed by a few attempts on Nena's part at a muted conversation. But from such a little nun it was impossible to pry more than two words in a row. She smiled and smiled—or at least it could be imagined that she did—and all that she finally said, stammering, was that in her opinion the monkey would surely come tonight, because "never more than three nights went by" (that is, he did not fail to appear at least every three nights).

And, sure enough, just at the crack of dawn, when a natural somnolence already weighed on their lids, a vague shadow appeared at the fanlight—a shadow which seemed for an instant enormous, then abruptly diminished in volume and assumed its proper shape.

Tombo first introduced between the iron bars the very long arm with which we are already familiar and waved it a bit, almost as though he were testing the air. Then he pushed through, shoulders first, and, from the architrave, measured the distance which separated him from the basin of an empty holy water stoup which rose to the right of the door; then he flung himself onto its brim with a very precise leap through the air. But since we are more or less familiar with his behavior under such circumstances, we shall not follow him step by step in his further evolutions, nor dwell upon his every little gesture and pose. That is, until the moment when, having crossed, swiftly and spiderlike, the entire length of the chapel, we find him clambering up the altar. Now Nena saw him right before her, just a few steps away, in the glaring light cast by the two large candles. Both she and the nun were petrified and held their breath. And then the horror began.

Tombo decisively approached the ciborium and opened it brusquely, slamming back the small door. He stood for a moment, peering inside with his head cocked, like a chicken, then

thrust in the usual arm and twice pulled out a handful of consecrated hosts, which he rapidly devoured. At this point the little
nun, unable to bear the sight of this sacrilege, made a sharp
movement and convulsively squeezed Nena's arm. Sensing that
her companion was preparing to intervene, also because she most
likely felt that the vigil's purpose had by now been achieved,
Nena nailed her to the spot with unsuspected energy, almost
with violence, at the same time clapping a hand over her mouth.
And the little nun submitted, either out of fear or temptation.

Tombo, having devoured the consecrated hosts, turned
around once or twice in a grotesque fashion at the edge of the
altar, as if he expected an audience's applause to follow his
performance. Then he approached the ciborium again and this
time took from it only one consecrated host, which he dropped
on the altar; then he pulled out the sacred chalice, holding it
horizontally by its stem, and this he also dropped, without even
bothering to look at it; next, with his right hand, he extracted
the sacred corporal, which, however, he held onto. Moving now
toward the cornice of the altar, he grasped with his left hand the
ampulla of holy wine, which he clutched to his chest. Back at
the center, he halted with an obtuse stare, holding these last two
objects in his hands, as if he did not know what to do with them,
or rather, since his hands were full, did not know how to proceed. Finally he violently shook out the sacred corporal, and
having in this way managed to unfurl it, flung it with a whip-
ping sound to his feet. Then he picked it up, at the same time
placing the ampulla between his legs, but an instant later he
again seized the ampulla and released the corporal—ending up
by holding them both, as at the start of the maneuver. But, due

to his jerky gestures, a part of the holy cloth had become wrapped around his forearm, and now Tombo realized that he could use his right hand without dropping the holy cloth. So he again seized the sacred chalice and, having shaken the ampulla to throw out the stopper, he prepared to fill it with the sacred wine. To accomplish this, he proceeded in a bizarre manner: without moving the flask away from his chest, he pulled the sacred chalice itself close to himself and the mouth of the flask; then, bending his whole body forward and contorting himself, he managed to pass a few drops of the sacred liquid from one receptacle to the other. That having been done, he squatted down and delicately set the sacred vessel between his feet. After this he got to his feet with an abrupt movement, brandished the ampulla with a sort of libidinous frenzy and licked its orifice; an instant later he had pushed the end of the flask into his mouth and was drinking the rest of the sacred wine, down to the last drop.

There was not much wine, and yet the effect was almost immediate. Without actually intoxicating him, it was enough to confer on the animal a great verve and boldness and on his gestures something even more brusque and farcical. Now the ampulla was discarded; having dropped it, Tombo thrust it away angrily with both hands. Once again he squatted down and took up the chalice, which he placed right at the center of the altar. He also picked up the host and laid it on top of the chalice, like a cover. Finally he snatched the corporal, which still dangled from his arm, not to cover the first two objects but to throw it slapdash over his shoulders. Thus vested, he circled around these objects with a dancelike step, jumping up and down with his feet together, several times, hectically, loudly slapping the altar's slab. Then he got around to the sacred chalice, which he seized, keeping his back to the pews, that is, looking toward the ciborium; he lifted it; put it down again; made a half turn, opened his arms, though holding his elbows close to his sides and with his palms open; turned again toward the chalice, lifting it again. . .For a moment the two women did not understand, they refused to understand. . . . Reader, do not condemn me: *Tombo was saying Mass.*

By now he was beastically devouring the consecrated host and drinking the sacred wine. And at this point I am gripped by another hesitation. I don't know whether I have the right to tell all and to disturb good souls to such an extent; but in the end I am compelled to report the final abomination of that abominable night. Seized by a sudden necessity, Tombo dropped the sacred chalice and let it roll on the altar's slab; and then, against a corner of the tabernacle. . .and I must find some way of saying it. . .he micturated on the altar.

The long restrained scream of the nun rang out. She flung herself on her knees and amidst convulsive sobs first cried and then barely murmured: "Oh God, forgive us!" As for the old maid, she did not utter a word. She rose to her feet in a daze and walked into the church.

Hearing that fracas, Tombo had hastened to throw everything back into the ciborium, whose door he slammed shut again. He undoubtedly recognized his mistress, and, running like a streak across the chapel, showing all the signs of insane terror, he left by the way he had come.

I shall avail myself of this moment of pause to advance an

hypothesis: that the monkey had, probably more than once, watched the sacrifice which tonight he had crudely and impiously imitated. As we know, it was his habit to go out at night; and it is also true that in some places and at certain seasons the first Mass is said when it is still dark. Therefore, Tombo had had an opportunity to observe the ceremony from behind the fanlight, if by chance he had lingered outside; until one fine night he had been taken by the whim of trying to imitate those celebrants. And that was his first and last attempt. But as I have remarked before, I do not claim to explain anything in this obscure story.

Since he had taken the quicker route, the animal got home before Nena. There he rushed back into his cage, pulled the door shut behind him (though this time he neglected to drop the latch) and slipped into his harness, though he got it twisted and too tight on one shoulder. When his returned mistress came into the kitchen, all of his limbs were seized by a violent tremor, yet nevertheless he flung himself down on his pallet and pretended to be asleep; but almost at once, as if convinced that such a ruse was futile, he opened his eyes again and stared at her beseechingly. Then he chittered faintly and made the gesture of tearing his hair, wishing perhaps by that act to confess his repentance. Nena did not say a word to him and acted as if she weren't even aware of his presence.

To the feverish questions of the two women who had remained behind, she simply said: "He must die."

6

Lilla, partly supported by Bellonia, tried with all of her meager forces to plead Tombo's case. Just as she had considered her sister's consternation at the beast's transgressions excessive, so now she thought excessive and cruel the projected punishment, which was the logical outcome of that consternation. Lamenting, sometimes even weeping a little, her bony face disfigured beyond what can be easily conceived by the average imagination, with her pince-nez awry, she pattered without a moment's rest after Nena, laboring to present arguments in favor of the monkey, arguments which in the end were always the same ones. Unwilling at first to give any explanations, Nena decided to yield and began to argue along lines that seemed quite normal; but she remained adamant, and the upshot was the usual endless discussions.

In substance Nena said that Lilla's very arguments made the monkey's case absolutely hopeless, and that precisely because Tombo was an animal he could and must be subjected to the fate of his peers. Animals, it is true, are entitled to the greatest indulgence, but only when it is a question of tolerable transgressions and venial sins. If they become harmful and dangerous, they must be destroyed. And this animal was not only harmful and dangerous, but something much worse—and here she avoided using the exact term. Besides—Lilla had said so herself— how could one control such a beast? If he didn't do one thing he'd do another, and whatever precautions were taken, he would think up something to get around them. Not to mention the fact that the two of them would become the talk of the entire city (that's what the old maid said), if they did not take quick and energetic steps; and not just the talk, but the very essence of opprobrium, and so outcasts in the eyes of all decent, God-fearing people. In fact—it is hard to explain how—a few hours after the event the story of the monkey who said Mass was being discussed all over the neighborhood. Other tenants, and almost completely unknown little old ladies, were already calling at the old maids' apartment, on one pretext or another. And we won't even mention all the traffic between their house and the convent.

These were Nena's arguments, and one can't say that they weren't better than her sister's, and bound to convince someone who, like Lilla, hadn't fully grasped how matters stood. For this lack of understanding, I might add in passing, I personally would not venture to blame the poor thing. Yet she, only half persuaded, could not resign herself. When, utterly surrendering, she unconsciously hit on the supreme argument and vaguely reminded Nena that Tombo was a sacred memento, indeed in a sense represented their dead brother, the latter retorted, almost spitefully, that Tombo was only a beast and did not represent anyone, and that if their brother were alive and had seen this beast perpetrate such an iniquity, he would certainly not hesitate to kill him. In the end, all that Lilla obtained was that, before executing the sentence and to set their consciences at rest, some holy man whom they both trusted would be consulted.

One of their habitual visitors, and perhaps also their spiritual director, was a certain elderly priest—or maybe he wasn't a priest but something even higher in the ecclesiastical hierarchy—Monsignor Tostini. To this man was entrusted the final word on the decision to be taken. But to say "the final word" is probably going too far: it is quite possible that Nena was reserving for herself the right to act as she wished even if the Monsignor were to pronounce himself against her; for the time being, however, it did not cost her anything to grant her sister that satisfaction and, besides, she knew with whom she was dealing.

Monsignor Tostini was—how shall I say?—a trifle deaf and had, as a result, a booming voice. He was one of those priests who like to think that they speak directly, without circumlocutions, and at the same time make a great show of tolerance and understanding for all human and non-human matters; who seem to value greatly and extol nature and all things created by our Lord; who pretend to look upon the failings of weak sinners with exemplary mildness; who must sometimes, alas, suffer outrages meekly; who have a sweet smile and speak about flights of swallows, church bells in the morning, their lungs expanding in the pure country air; who, on all occasions, wish to appear disposed to indulgence. In a word, one of those priests of whom people say: "Now there's a holy man, he really follows in Christ's footsteps!"—the typical specimen of a breed which none other can surpass in bombast and backwardness.

Brought into the green living room, this Monsignor listened to both parties. Then, without immediately pronouncing himself and after some groans of doubtful interpretation, he launched into a speech which, from its very outset, was full of feeling, though its scope was so broad that one could not tell exactly where it was headed. It was, however, meant to praise

God, through his creatures and in a general sort of way. But he was still picking his way through the exordium, when someone knocked at the door. It was another priest, whom the old maids called Father Alessio, *tout court*. He could still be considered a youth, ordained at the most the year before; blond and blue eyed. A timid priest who blushed easily and who, people already said, was very charitable, although he had lived in the town only a short time. He was a foreigner, a Swiss if I'm not mistaken. He had come to call for reasons which had nothing to do with those which had convoked the court in the living room, and of which he was unaware. Nonetheless, it seemed in place to ask him into the living room and, after having briefly informed him of the matter, invite him to take part in the debate.

Tostini, who did not know him, was somewhat annoyed by the interruption, which occurred just when his eyes were beginning to become moist. When calm was re-established, he resumed his speech, but with such vast and unexpected ramifications that Lilla, who trembled for Tombo's fate, gathered the courage to interrupt him when he paused to hawk into his handkerchief. Almost stuttering, she asked him whether he thought the monkey had to be killed. The Monsignor, driven into a corner, moaned and groaned but in the end was forced to pronounce himself. And he pronounced himself more or less in the following terms, leaving out, of course, the many meanderings of his eloquence:

There are sins that can and must be forgiven, even some of the mortal sins. For instance, no one can fail to see that, horrible and dreadful as the sin of gluttony is, it is possible to find a way to excuse, if not to justify it: and in truth, to pay homage, even excessively, to the feast laid out by God is not always an irreparable fault. (This rather unorthodox magnanimity on Tostini's part was not totally disinterested. But we'll skip further elaboration on this point.) But for those sins which no decent soul can look upon without trembling, it is a different matter altogether. Unspeakable sins; sins for which no remission can be hoped either from our Lord or from men; the sins which Dante had in mind when he said: "here mercy can live when it is quite dead". . .the sins, in general and in particular, which offend the majesty of our Lord; and which all belong to a single and abominable category. To crush such sins and sinners is a glorious act. Where would the world, society and the individual end up if there existed souls so cowardly, or at any rate if they were the majority, as to tolerate this kind of sin? Now then, the monkey, insofar as he was an animal was no doubt entitled to greater indulgence; but, at the same time, precisely insofar as he was an animal, greater severity was admissable and excessive scruples could be excluded. For God created the beasts as man's subjects and for his convenience. Therefore, the two exceptions cancelled each other out. "Not only was the consecrated host shattered," Tostini ended, with a cry, "but it was shattered by bestial teeth! The altar of Christ has been befouled!" The conclusion was clear: thumbs down.

Lilla swooned. Nena's demeanor remained wholly composed and natural, indicating that there was nothing strange in a sensible person taking that stand. Yet she also looked slightly distracted, and distractedly, for the sake of politeness, she asked Father Alessio for his opinion.

"Yes, yes," Tostini agreed benevolently, "what does my dear brother in Christ think of this?"

The young priest, who until then had remained deferentially silent, blushed deeply and shifted in his chair, clearing his throat timidly.

"Well, I don't know," he said, with a marked foreign accent, "but. . .but it seems to me that the monkey is innocent."

"What?" three voices cried out in unison, or rather four, since Bellonia had in the meantime slipped into the room and sat down next to the door. As for Tostini, he cried "What?" because he actually hadn't heard, and indeed cupped his hand around his ear, smiling obtusely.

"Yes. . . ," Father Alessio resumed, startled, "I mean. . . it's not his fault."

"You mean to say that what the monkey has done is not his fault?" said the Monsignor, who had heard this time, with unruffled benevolence. "Yes and no. I understand what you're trying to say: a monkey is an unknowing brute. Nevertheless, anyone who sins is a sinner. Besides, don't forget that when a priest forgives a sin (and not all sins can be forgiven, as I have explained before) he does not do so for nothing or, as we say, *gratis et amore Dei.* Though in harmony with the precept which reads: 'The Lord does not desire the sinner's death, but rather that he repent and live,' we always try, and always should try, to crush the sin instead of the sinner; it is no less true that the forgiven sin is forgiven on certain conditions, that its expiation, its proper punishment, must follow. And this never fails, and is all the more dreadful when it occurs only in the sinner's soul. Eh, it would be a fine thing if any sin at all, any offense to the

Eternal, to the Lord of all and everything, went unavenged! But here, my dear young man, in exchange for what would we forgive this animal for its iniquitous sin? Who do you think should pay for it, eh? Now just try," Tostini added, with paternal joviality, "just try to spread the Gospel among the monkeys! I say this simply to meet you halfway, at least to the point of admitting that the sinner's conversion *per se* is sufficient to redeem the sin. And yet, I ask again, should or should not this conversion be at least accompanied by great pangs of conscience? Which are. . .the punishment. . .ahem, ahem. . .and which, in the case at hand, can not. . .ahem. . .take place. Is that clear?"

Since his speech was getting out of hand, the Monsignor stopped to catch his breath. Besides, it must be said that he was impatiently awaiting the coffee, for around that time of day he felt a trifle faint; but in the gravity of the moment the women had forgotten about it.

"Well, what do you say, my dear young man?" he added.

Father Alessio could feel his ears redden indecorously. He felt that if he spoke he would stammer. He was also a bit afraid of what he might say, and Tostini's paternal tone irritated him; so he shifted on his chair, coughing weakly, and did not say a word. But that's not how Tostini saw it. "Well, my dear young man? Speak up, speak freely," he repeated. No doubt the young priest's timidity amused him and confirmed him in his assurance.

"Well," said Alessio at last, stammering as he had foreseen, but with a faint note of irritation in his voice, which he had foreseen only in part, "Well, you are again speaking of sin. . . you said before that the monkey is entitled to greater indulgence. But why only greater? Rather, to all possible indulgence. What does a poor monkey know about your altars and your consecrated hosts? . . ."

"Father!" cried Nena.

"Father!" cried Lilla.

Bellonia muttered something under her breath. Monsignor Tostini wasn't quite sure that he'd actually heard the last sentence and cried, "What? what?" . . .craning forward and still smiling, just to be on the safe side. Actually, Father Alessio's expression was rather strong, but he had uttered it only because a more felicitous one hadn't come to him, and with an intention which he went on to explain.

All of them, after a pause, cried: "*Your* altars, *your* hosts!"

"But, of course. . .I meant to say *ours*. . .I said *yours* just referring to those which you, Monsignor, had spoken of"—and here the young man sighed with deep-felt emotion.

"Well, well, let's not go into it," Tostini said, still benevolent. "But I have already answered, it seems to me, this objection. Agreed, the monkey did not know what he was doing, but at this rate. . . . To get to the point, a horrible sin has been committed. Who, I ask once more, must pay for it, in your opinion? What are we to do with this sin, my boy? You certainly don't have any hope that the monkey will repent? And God, my boy, is infinitely merciful and good, but he is also a righteous God and just as he gives so much for so much, he also demands so much for so much."

The two "my boy's" had irritated Father Alessio even more than the many "my dear young man's"; nevertheless, gripping the arms of his chair, he managed to speak softly.

"Yes, but. . .besides, that's not what I meant. And in any case. . .after all, it's man who invented sin."

"What's that? What's that?" cried Nena, who had heard him quite clearly; and Lilla echoed her.

"Please, my dear ladies, don't get excited!" Tostini intervened, losing a trifle of his smile. "My young brother and fellow priest could be right, if by invented he means committed. There's no doubt that man had no need to sin to be happy in Eden; indeed, with his disobedience, he has prepared for himself a lifetime and in certain cases—God save us all from such a fate—an eternity of torment. Nevertheless the concept, the notion of sin comes to us directly and precisely from God; after all, from whom else could it come? Didn't He, by means of His Divine Son, teach us what is good and what is evil? Did not He grant us the ability to choose freely between one and the other? And in so doing, my dear young man, He has drawn our attention to sin (so that we should beware of it), to sin which prevents us from acting according to His intentions. . . ."

"Yes, but," Father Alessio repeated, gaining courage as his irritation mounted, "but what has a monkey got to do with all this? Your, I mean to say our, morality, may perhaps be all right for men, but not for animals. Animals do not have. . .our famous free will."

"*Perhaps. . .famous. . .*indeed!" The Monsignor grunted, losing another ounce of his smile. "But how many times, my blessed child, must I say it," he resumed, scanning his words in a singsong, "that the sin would subsist even if by chance the sinner did not exist. And our sacrosanct duty is to extirpate it no matter under which guise it manifests itself and no matter by which means. Here we have a sinner—even if he does not know that he has sinned—and I say if. . . . Now look, you're even confusing me. Besides, now that I come to think of it, what do you mean by declaring that animals do not have free will? You don't, I hope, mean to say that if the monkey has committed his horrible crime, he has done so by God's will? Because beings who do not possess free will can only follow the will of God: the Devil's will only counts in the hearts of men—unfortunately, it does count. Now, my boy, would you dare to assert such a possibility?"

"I don't care, and yet. . ."

"You don't care! And what don't you care about, may I ask?"

But this ridiculous interruption, due to Tostini's partial deafness, had a magical effect on Father Alessio. Everything which he had swallowed at the start of the conversation, and everything which had not yet seemed to him completely clear, suddenly came to his lips with unexpected and unrestrainable violence; the young man was set free. Forced to raise his voice a tone higher, and with his vocal chords and his brain kindling each other (so that the expression of his ideas acquired a vehemence which was new even to him), he became more and more excited and at last attained a state of drunken elation.

7

"What do you mean—*and yet,*" Nena had asked coldly. "What are you saying? Do you realize that you are blas-

pheming?" Lilla had timidly ventured. And Bellonia grumbled
something to show her indignation. While Tostini, completely
at sea, still thought it might help to regard the young man with
an ironic air. Pressed from all sides, the young priest burst out
with nearly childish vexation and obstinacy.

"I'm blaspheming? So much the worse if I am! But I'm
not blaspheming, you needn't worry. Instead, you, all of you,
are blaspheming. What God are you talking about? God is not
what you think He is. God is, Monsignor, just like myself, just
like that monkey, alien to your complicated accounts of give and
take! God has nothing to do with your or, let's say, our moral
institutions, our altars, our consecrated hosts. I'm not saying that
He is above or below these things. I say, however, that they do
not belong to Him, that they are not pertinent to Him or at least
no more so than any other thing, any other quality of man, beast
or star. God is not a god of justice. He is not merciful either. He
is not bad and He is not good. . ."

All exclaimed at once: "God is not good!"

"No, He is not good just as He is not bad. Your moral
standards, Monsignor, do not apply to Him. God is not so de-
graded as to know good and evil. I said that it was man who
invented sin, and then, out of cowardice, I remained silent when
you objected. Well, what you chose to understand is not what
I intended to say. I say that man has invented the very concept
of sin, and this is his greatest, indeed, his only sin. You talk of
free will! But do you realize that this, this is the real blasphemy,
your belief in free will? Don't you know that free will negates
God, as none of your so-called sins ever could, that is if they
existed. . ."

"Not at all, free will affirms God, because. . ."

"No, let me say what I've got to say—your canonical arguments have no place here. Free will negates God not because of the reasons which you have been taught to refute. It negates Him by the very fact that it limits Him—limits Him, I might say, in space. Let us suppose that God said to man: these are the two paths, follow one or the other—and here we won't mention the respective rewards and punishments which you have so foolishly played at inventing—and let us suppose that man decides to follow the path of evil. Very well: in what terms, with what means, I ask you, within what bounds could he follow it? Must he not, in order to do it, make use of that which God Himself has given him? Don't all the impulses of his heart come from God, as do all the instruments of his actions? Are not all these things part of God? But no, that doesn't suit you, because then God would be responsible for evil. So according to you, there must be a path which does not pass through God, and things which elude His dominion. Nor does it help to invoke the stupid sophism that these things elude God's dominion precisely because that is His will in the matter. How would such a will exist? It would only exist if God were something apart from His creatures, if God were not in all created things—as you yourselves admit He is—if God, in other words, were not God. And instead the whole universe is His living body. And there is only one thing that God Himself cannot do: deliver His creatures. . .because His creatures are nothing but Himself, and He is nothing but His creatures. God Himself cannot deny Himself without ceasing to be God, indeed without ceasing to be anything at all. All does not have the power to become

nothing, even though nothing can become all. God who ceases
to become God, who ceases to be! That is just a ridiculous play
on words. But that's not how matters stand, Monsignor. . ."

"But God. . ."

"God—I don't know what God is. A hundred times each
day I curse Him and a hundred times I bless Him. . . I don't
know what He is, and perhaps for that very reason I am closer
to Him. Sometimes I imagine Him as the general or abstract
idea of all the countless things which are on earth, since the
earth is all I know. The abstract idea of that hat of yours resting
on the table is what binds it to all other conceivable hats; and
so God would be that which binds and unites each thing to each
other thing—the flower to the bird, the moon to the palm of my
hand—that in which every conflict finds peace and all that is
heterogeneous becomes homogeneous, while still remaining different. He would be what these objects have in common between
them; and all that there is in common between what we call
hate and what we call love, pride and humility. That is why I
was saying before that God is unaware of good and evil, that one
cannot call Him good or bad. He does not fit into any moral
category, because nothing is outside of Him and He embraces
everything. Therefore, everything comes to us from Him, the
so-called good just as the evil, without distinction. . ."

"Jesus help us!"

"Have mercy!"

"Saints above!"

"No, no, don't be alarmed, these are not blasphemies. I'm
saying that evil is not evil perhaps, that all is good. But it's not
that either—I don't know what I'm trying to say. . .God, I search

for Him. . .well, yes, even what we call evil comes to us from Him: this is how I worship Him! I search for Him; this is man's way to worship—the other way means to lose Him forever. I search for Him incessantly, without rest. I know I shall not lose Him because I shall never find Him. And I cannot find Him— because I am He, and when I say I search for Him, I mean I try to be as much as possible He. . .I know what you think: that I'm contradicting myself, because the other way of worshipping also comes to us from Him and is He. . .I myself have said that everything is He. But I don't care if I contradict myself, and, besides, I'm not contradicting myself; it's just that I lack the words to say what I want to say and I am forced to fall back on your, or our, terms. I'm aware that worshipping, according to my idea of God, doesn't mean anything—how can one worship oneself, while being oneself?—since I am God, just like all other created things? By saying that I search for Him, perhaps I just mean that I am He already, with all that He contains, all that He is, of good and evil. . .and not even the word "creation" has more meaning. You cannot speak of created things if God *is* the created things, that and no more. God has created nothing. God is. I am. Everything is. Or, since in this context our distinctions no longer have any value, He is not, and I am not, and all is not: Or even, nothingness is; or it is not. Whichever way you like.

"I also try to negate Him. I wish I could reach the point of knowing if He is or is not—again I am forced to fall back on our words—which would be the loftiest way of worshipping Him. But I can't succeed. Because how could I negate Him without making use of what He has given me—without at least being?

And by being, I affirm Him. I try to imagine Him, as though that were possible. I remember that at the seminary up North, one of my companions had written some sort of story and God appeared in it—as a newborn child. A newborn child? Why not? Or an old, bearded man, it's all the same. I adore Him in all His creatures, which are part of Him and me. In all of His forms, each of which is perfect. I know about all the other infinite forms that man, in his pride, thinks he can invent; but it would be an illusion to think that they are more perfect or that they are not God. They are only different, less manifest forms of God. Each form is perfect in itself: therefore, it could not exist in any other way. I know I'm speaking obscurely and that I keep contradicting myself; but that doesn't matter to me, so long as it is the truth. How many times have I found myself kneeling before a cat washing its face, before a squirrel—there was one at the presbytery—eating a nut, before a toad in the sun that is startled and freezes in mid-stride with one leg still stretched behind it and, looks and listens without moving. Or before any other thing, before a blade of grass as well as the house of a man, before the stars of the sky as well as the refuse from a living body. You see, I tell myself, this cat is the way it is and cannot be any other way, and it is perfect; another thing or form could never be a more perfect or beautiful cat than this, or would only be another thing, it would not be a cat. But this other thing would be equally perfect in itself. I have no hope that I can make you understand me. I could perhaps, with other words, but then you would understand me, that's just it; and that would be proof that I was lying. . . . Well, Monsignor, these are my infinite altars: not mine, but those of all men of good will—as you'd call them. Among these altars the meanest and most melancholy is the altar before which your priests genuflect.

"Some people have thought that man sins because evil and pain are more pleasing to him than good and his own good, or that evil is just as necessary to him as good. Blind and presumptuous affirmation! What evil and what good? Man sins only because he cannot help but sin; but, naturally, he does not sin. Nor can evil be more pleasing and necessary to him than good. Indeed it cannot even be necessary to him because it is, like good, he himself. And it is he himself because it is God Himself. There is no evil and there is no good. Good and evil exist because God only *is*. And they are like one thing, not one against the other. They too are the living body of God—God and nothing more."

The young priest had risen to his feet while he was speaking. Now he fell back into his seat with a crash, and a shadow seemed to darken his brow and the fire in his eyes. There was a brief pause. His listeners were breathless. Then Father Alessio became animated again, but with a different, sadder excitement.

"Forgive me," he resumed, "if I have talked about myself; or rather, forgive me if I have talked to you about God, a subject bound to displease you. . . . And so, the monkey has eaten the consecrated host, the monkey has said Holy Mass. So what, I ask you? Cannot everyone say Mass, if he likes to and if he really feels he must? What creature's homage and worship, to use your language, can fail to find grace before the throne of its Creator? Hasn't the monkey, even before this, perhaps eaten the body of God every day? Doesn't everyone eat it every day? I know only too well that you will kill this being which seems to you deformed and unclean, this being which is as sacred and divine as God, of whom he is part; that you will kill him for a horrible misdeed which in him is only a natural impulse. But if you do, that will just be proof that so it must be, that so it shall be, undoubtedly. God—still using your language—who inspired the monkey to say Mass, will also inspire you with the coward-ice, the blindness, the shame of your—and here it really fits—your misdeed. The monkey has made water all over the altar: and so what? God. . ."

But at this point Tostini finally found his voice again, and the others with him; the strange spell, which they themselves could not fathom, was broken.

"Enough, boy!" the Monsignor yelled, half rising from his chair. "Enough is enough! I have been able to keep silent as long as you were engaged in your obscure, certainly not com-mendable, speculations, but which I, ahem, might even excuse in an inexperienced and too ardent young man, ahem, ahem. . . . What am I saying, *excuse?*" he suddenly resumed, howling like a madman. "What am I saying! God forgive me! *Inexperienced . . .ardent. . .*indeed! You are tempted by the Devil! No, not tempted, you have already yielded to his temptation, to his flattery! You are his prey. You are casting doubt on the sacro-sanct truth of faith, you are blaspheming like the most miserable, like the most impious of scoundrels, you. . . . This is the truth. And I, I must—for I would be betraying my most sacred duties if I didn't—I must report this to the proper authorities. And now, my boy, as your superior, as a priest, as a man, I order you to remain silent!"

And Tostini dropped back into his chair, gasping and hissing like a kettle.

"Enough yourself, with your gibberish, by God! And with your *my boy's*—luckily, at least, I'm no longer your *dear young man!* I may be young, but you are the living proof that old age is not always accompanied by wisdom, that is something I had to tell you sooner or later. Go and report to anyone you like, that's the kind of sin you can handle! But you know what to do with that other sin, too, unfortunately. . . . Why didn't I tell you a little while ago when you were asking me, with all those hems and haws, and other disgusting grunts, what we were supposed to do with this sin, *my boy?*"—and Father Alessio aped the Monsignor's voice and tone—"Why didn't I tell you to shove it down your pocket, by the blood of your God, not to mention up your behind! Report to anyone you like—I insist on it—go and confess what you've heard today. Ask permission of your superiors even to make peepee, with or without a candle. . . ."

Tostini lurched back on the armchair, red as a turkey, clutching his hand to his heart. "I'm stifling!" he murmured.

The scandal had reached its height. Father Alessio's blasphemies and outrages, and above all his unheard-of vulgarity, were becoming intolerable even to himself. He had not actually lost his head, indeed he had acquired a sort of coldness; but he enjoyed being vulgar, he wanted to be vulgar, he felt he had to. Doing violence to his urbane nature, he forced himself to be as vulgar as possible and, if he hadn't been even more vulgar, it was only because he didn't know how.

The two old maids, followed by Bellonia, had now gotten to their feet. Strange or not strange to say, the most indignant was Lilla, whose cause, in fact, the young man was in his own way pleading; she, however, could not find words and, with tears in her eyes, continually adjusting her pince-nez, trembled from top to toe. Nena, for an instant undecided, stared at the young priest who had also risen, and her lips were trembling, too. Bellonia emitted a series of stifled clucks, hastily crossing herself again and again. While Tostini, still holding his hand over his heart, now murmured: "The sacred viand. . .so, the sacred viand. . .the outrage of the sacred viand. . ."

"I don't give a screw for your sacred viand!" Father Alessio declared in a frigid voice, uttering the scurrilous sentence with a visible effort.

"Leave this house immediately!" Nena finally said.

"Out of this house!" repeated Lilla, in a whisper.

"Away! Away! Out! Out!" Bellonia exclaimed in turn.

"I'll be delighted," Father Alessio retorted. "But before I go, I have something else to say to you. And just to you, you bemustached and corrupt old hag. Why is your sister trembling and not saying a word? Why does she tremble just to look at you, and not only today? Just like that monkey, poor woman. . ."

"I'm not tre-embl-ing at all," Lilla blubbered.

"Anyway," the young man continued, without paying any attention to her, "why do you want to kill the monkey? What are, I want to know, your real reasons?" And he stared at Nena with an insane glare in his eyes.

"I've already begged you to leave," she replied with calm dignity. "And if you were, if not a priest, at least a man, I would point out to you that you possess perhaps the second of the cardinal virtues, but not the third and definitely not the first and fourth."

"This is a joke, a ridiculous riddle!" the young priest burst out, perplexed, despite himself, by her singular mode of expression, and, inevitably, a trifle deflated. "This is an absurdity worthy of you. As if I knew the four cardinal virtues in order! Why, I don't even know them out of order! The four cardinal virtues, phooey!" He stopped to search for a vulgar phrase, but did not find it. "Why don't you answer my question?" he finally continued, having regained his assurance.

"Now how must I tell you to leave this house?"

"Yes, leave," Tostini, who had finally revived a bit, weakly came to her support.

"I'm leaving! I'm leaving!" screamed Father Alessio, ramming his hat on his head. "Now, go ahead, sacrifice that poor creature, that monkey, sacrifice me, go ahead and sacrifice, as you've always done, sacrifice God's whole world to. . . . Revenge yourself. Revenge yourself for your shame, your ridiculous impotence, your rancor, your rage. Revenge yourself for not having been chosen by a man, with whom you would have wallowed in all sorts of filthy pleasures. But love, the modest love which God inspires among men, you hate it, and that is why no one has chosen you; and that is why—with your hopeless jealousy— you've prevented your sister from experiencing the pleasure of being held by a man's arms, of feeling on her lips the . . ."

"Oh, Jesus have mercy!"

"And what's wrong with that? That was her right. Everyone has the right to happiness, and God has so arranged things that—whatever your blasphemous priests may claim—there is some in *this* world. Do you perhaps think that your sister would not be closer to God if . . .even now, even now! Revenge yourself for. . .Oh Lord, save her, deliver this poor creature from the others, from herself, from her putrid chastity! . . .So revenge yourself for. . ."

"Oh blessed God! Oh Lord, Thy blessed will be done! . . ."

"Enough, enough!"

"Out, out!"

And Bellonia interrupted the young man's wild, frenetic speech, actually pushing him out by his elbows. Father Alessio, as if he had suddenly gone off the boil, waved his hand, shrugged, and left. Bellonia followed him all the way out to the stairs, and slammed the door after him.

Nena was covering her eyes with her hand. Tostini, still utterly prostrated, did not lift his. There was a moment of profound and consternated silence. Then, shrill and loud, hysterically, rose Lilla's voice.

"Oh Lord, have pity on us!"

And here all of them, joined at last by the Monsignor, began to exclaim, to scream, to outshout each other, and here we'll leave the assemblage to its outcries!

But poor Tombo! He couldn't have hit upon a worse lawyer for his defense.

8

Yes, kill him, but how? The best way, Lilla said, was to give him to a. . .yes, to one of those organizations which painlessly. . . . No, they'd hurt him anyway, Nena retorted, pacing up and down the room and wringing her hands in her usual fashion. Ever since this whole story had begun the old maids appeared more rumpled than ever, because they often forgot to put on their hairnets and their wispy hair, standing on end or hanging limply, was yellowish and smoky white. Anyway, they'll hurt the poor beast! "So," was Bellonia's comment, meaning that after all that wouldn't be the end of the world. "So—a jab in his throat won't hurt him at all." The good maid was used to killing chickens.

What about an unexpected blow on the head with a club? Or a crack at the base of the neck as they do with rabbits? Or a clout with a hammer as they do with cattle? Or a loop around the throat? What about holding his head under water as they often do with pigeons? Or what if we put the whole cage into the water like a mousetrap? Yes, but where would we find a large enough tub? . . .and they went on forever, and without realizing it, they labored to invent the most refined tortures for the un-lucky animal. No, no, the thing to do is to send him to one of those organizations. . .But I'm telling you that they'd hurt him anyway! Besides, he'd understand that he's going to die; no, no. . . .

Two days had passed since Tombo had been caught in the chapel. The first day he had continued to show an insane fear and had been as good and humble as he could; on the second, when he saw that nothing was happening to him, he grew more and more assured and regained some of his customary vivacity. But now, seeing that council of women in front of his cage, he again became suspicious; perhaps he even understood some of their words, since, taking it for granted that he could not comprehend human speech, they did not abstain from using his name. In any case, the beast instinctively recognized the truth of that sad and ineluctable proverb which says: "Council of foxes, slaughter of chickens," and he turned his eyes apprehensively from one old maid to the other (he attached less importance to Bellonia, for he was well aware of her position in the house), scrutinizing their faces, wailing faintly and every so often making a frenzied circuit of his cage.

Night was falling; the kitchen, squalid like all kitchens when the stove is not lit and no one is moving about preparing a meal, was immersed in a funereal twilight. Nena spoke, continuing to pace up and down with her waddling step; ridiculous in her senile obesity; wearing a short vest, but without a skirt. She spoke, at once feverish and dreamy:

"When your dog has served you for many years and must die; when you want to get rid of him or he has sinned; when his skin is covered with scabs and minute animals, his ears are frazzled and bleeding, his nose is always dry and he drags his hind legs, limply hanging to one side, like dead things; or when the sight of him has become unbearable to you, do not entrust this dog who was your friend to the hands of a stranger, not even to the hands of your brother; he does not know him as you do; don't let him sense that he is dying, don't deprive him of this last token of respect: you yourself must be the one who puts him to death. Call him to a corner of the garden, give him the last bone to gnaw, caress his head with one hand and with the other, without his noticing. . . . This is, I think, what I once read. I myself will kill him, if that's how it must be. And I also remem-

ber having read, long ago, about a peasant who killed a traveler
to steal his watch, and at the moment he struck he said to him:
'Forgive me, brother. . .' It's ridiculous, isn't it? It's ridiculous, I
mean, that I should remember all these things now. . .But
enough. Yes, I will do it with my own hands: now I know
how. . .But what am I crying about, fool that I am! And you,
why are you standing there like dummies? You are crying, too,
my poor sister. . .But enough, I said. Come, put on the light,
and caress him, kiss him, say good-bye to him, and above all he
must not worry! Come, get busy. . .Now, right away: I've
found the way, now you'll see."

"No, not right away," Lilla whimpered. "Can't we wait
till tomorrow?"

"Tomorrow? Why tomorrow? It would be worse," Nena
replied, and left the kitchen.

Soon after she called the others into her room and showed
them a long hatpin, one of those objects which in respectable
families are handed down from generation to generation. It was
a pin in an antique style; a pin of gold, terminating at one end
in a kind of trefoil set at an angle, with a faintly reddish stone
imbedded in one of its lobes, not a ruby, however; it was, given
its use, extremely sharp.

"See, with this it will take just a moment."

But, unfortunately, despite their precautions the monkey
must have noticed something. All that bustle did not promise
any good. They had put on the lights, closed the window,
placed the cage on the floor so as to clear the large table on which
it usually stood and on which the operation was to take place.
Then, having let out the prisoner, they had first given him a

succulent tidbit, one of his favorites. And now they were caressing Tombo, as they did sometimes, tickling his belly, his chest where he had almost no fur, holding him down with his back against the table and his arms spread open, just like Dante's Caiphas; they addressed him by his most endearing nicknames. But he would not be deceived and turned his eyes rapidly, now desperate, now beseeching, between the two who held him, that is, Lilla and Bellonia. He wailed loudly, wrinkled his forehead, tried to shake them off, to turn over, but, mainly thanks to Bellonia, couldn't succeed. He even tried to bite her since he felt she was gripping him more firmly (but also because, of the two, she was the maid). And yet, it was quite clear that he didn't want to displease them by seeming not to appreciate their games, and was trying as much as possible to check such manifestations of his instincts—almost as though he did not hold them responsible for the terror and dismay by which he felt overwhelmed. Despite his anguish, one could sense that in his heart he had thrown himself on their mercy; he was even trustful, no matter what might come to him from those wills stronger than his own—as it is with all animals, this being the sole weapon left them against human wickedness. But perhaps he did not really believe that his situation was so serious. At this point Lilla broke down and, using as an excuse "something that didn't agree with her," let go her hold; nevertheless she remained there, wandering dazedly about the kitchen.

Killing him was not a matter of just a moment. Now Tombo sensed only too clearly that he was to die. Nena, holding her weapon behind her back, had approached him, and she too fondled and petted him with her free hand. Then she crossed herself rapidly and stroked him again, at the same time holding his legs—Bellonia was taking care of his arms. And suddenly she struck. But, as one could have predicted, the hatpin did not follow the desired path: it penetrated a trifle higher or lower than the heart, or encountered a rib. It was necessary to repeat the blow once, twice, three times. A tomblike silence had fallen; which was torn by Lilla's hysterical scream, a sentence howled out precipitously, almost a single word: "We're killing our brother!"

"Shut up, ninny!" Nena snapped, between gritted teeth; and this was the first and last time she ever said such a thing to her sister.

At last Tombo, who had struggled furiously, expired; the violence of his jerks died, his eyes died, his eyes which at the final moment expressed nothing but dismayed wonderment. The wounds did not bleed; but a thin trickle of blood came from the corner of his mouth.

The following day Nena had a small box made which was suited to that tiny body, lined with zinc like those for human beings. She put him inside and carefully sealed it. Since the evening before, she had relapsed into one of her spells of mutism, and when Lilla mourned for Tombo, she had to do so in secret with the maid. Nena simply announced that it would be a good idea to take a trip to their home town to see to their affairs, and that she was planning to leave the next day. The reason she gave looked very much like a pretext; however, she left early in the morning.

And at their home town, in a corner of the garden attached to their old house, in the earth which spring was beginning to crack and at the foot of a young walnut tree which was putting out its first leaves, she buried Tombo with all the honors.

It was a mild day; a smell of sage and the clucking of chickens came from the nearby kitchen gardens; the sun was just beginning to sting. And in that distant place, I hope, the hero of this story still rests in peace.

EPILOGUE

Of the few characters herein encountered, some, like Bellonia and Monsignor Tostini, are prolonging a decrepit old age; and some, like the two old maids, are already dead. It seems incredible, and perhaps it actually is, but such is the usual conclusion. Imperceptibly stooping and growing colder we approach our beginning—so sang (or croaked) the poet. Anyway, we've had more than one day to become used to this; is not this a world in which incredible things take place and, I would say, only incredible things?

Father Alessio could not say Mass for a long time. This may seem a small matter, but, as luck would have it, during that same period, I mean at the time of his brainstorm in the old maids' house, he contracted some sort of mental illness which gave rise to fears for his sanity, and liver trouble, too; so that "his superiors" were quite happy to seize this opportunity and avoid a greater scandal. Why he didn't defrock himself, is another matter. But in the meantime he too has grown older.

The graveyard of T. is not far from town and the dusty

carriage road. One can also get there by a twisting short cut, bordered here and there by dry stone walls over which one can see olive groves, cultivated fields, the peasants' small houses. But, either because at that spot the horizon is naturally cramped, or God knows for what other reason, one has no feeling at all of being in the country, in our Lord's vast countryside. First of all, before reaching the open country, one passes behind certain houses sunk below the road and with their facades on the opposite side; then, higher up, on one side the hill falls sheerly to the road, and there is even a contorted olive tree which juts over it so low that one must be careful not to bump one's head. And the shrubs beyond the narrow valley are equally sad and faded.

Inside the graveyard the horizon is balked and encircled by huge eucalyptus trees with shining, scaly trunks, which always seem to ooze a sickly sweat, and also by an almost ruined retaining wall. On one side all that one can see is the arid, bluish hump of a mountain. On these eucalyptus and cypress trees— their innocent neighbors—there sometimes alights and whistles an agitated thrush or a more placid blackbird; but here the magpies live and flutter all year round. A melancholy population! Afflicted by some mysterious hypochondria and natural languishment, they fly and emit their song as all birds do; but when they croak, a brief, fluid croak of sonorous consonants, they do so in a weary, hopeless tone; and when they fly, theirs is a drooping flight, laboriously resumed just when it is about to fall to the ground. They bear a strange resemblance, chiefly because of that whirring sound, to a man trudging through the streets of a city during the dog days. They do not seem to have any commerce with other birds. And when, God knows how, a lively jay bird happens to alight on one of those trees, its screeches sound like those of a child crying in a house deserted or struck by misfortune, and the very air of this somnolent world is shaken. But, of course, a mocking and exuberant jay cannot be befriended by a gathering of magpies; and so he soon goes back to the sowed fields, the oaks and apples trees.

Here in fact are buried the two old maids, who, so I hope, are resting in peace. And to anyone who looks about him, it seems that an impalpable gray dust has fallen on everything.

Translated by Raymond Rosenthal

Wedding Night

A T THE END of the wedding banquet the chimney sweep
was announced. The father, out of joviality, and because
it seemed proper to him that a ceremony such as the cleaning of
the chimney should be celebrated on just that day, gave the order
to let him come in. But the man did not appear; he preferred to
remain in the kitchen, where the great hearth was. Not all the
toasts had yet been given, and this was why some of the guests,
in their heart of hearts, criticized the interruption; nonetheless,
due to the uproar made by the children, everyone rose from the
table.

The bride had never seen a chimney sweep: she had been in
boarding school when he used to come. Going into the kitchen
she saw a tall, rather corpulent man, with a serious gray beard
and bent shoulders; he was dressed in a corduroy suit the color
of linseed oil. His stoop was counterbalanced by the weight of
two huge mountain boots which, seemed to hold his entire body

erect. Although he had just washed very carefully, the skin of his face was deeply tinted with black, as though many black-heads of varying dimensions had taken root there; a black deposit, gathered between the lines of his forehead and cheeks, conferred a quality of meditative wisdom on that physiognomy. But this impression quickly dissolved, and the man's great timidity became quite obvious, especially when his features broke into a sort of smile.

He nearly frightened the young bride, because he was standing behind the door, though he acted frightened himself; and, as if he had been caught doing something reprehensible and had to justify his presence in that place, he began to repeat, speaking directly to the young bride, some sentences which she did not hear or did not understand. He stammered insistently and behaved as if he thought that what he said concerned her greatly and, all the while, he looked at her with the eyes of a beaten dog and yet significantly. From the very first moment the young bride was aware of his caterpillar nature.

He took off his jacket and began to unbutton his vest. She slipped out through the other door, but continued to follow what was going on in the kitchen; she had the feeling that something improper was about to happen and that her presence might make him uneasy in the performance of his rites. Somehow she almost felt ashamed for him. But there was no noise to feed her imagination and so she went back in again. The children had been sent away and he was alone. At that moment he was climbing a ladder set up inside the hood of the fireplace; his feet were bare and he was in his shirtsleeves, a brown shirt. Across his chest, fastened with leather straps, he had a tool which resembled the scraper for a kneading trough but whose use remained forever unknown to the young bride. And he had a kind of black gag, tied up behind his ears, which fitted over his mouth and nose. But she did not see him enter the flue of the chimney, because she ran away again.

When she came back the second time, the kitchen was empty and a strange smell, a terrible smell, had spread through it. Looking around her, the young bride connected it first with the man's large shoes set in a corner next to a bundle of clothes; it was, however, the death smell of the soot which was piling up on the hearthstone, falling in intermittent showers to the rhythm of a dull scraping which gnawed at the marrow of the house and which she felt echoing in her own entrails. In the intervals, a muffled rubbing revealed the man's laborious ascent.

An instant of absolute silence fell, an instant of lacerating suspense for the young bride. She continued to stare at the mouth of the flue, there under the hood at the end of the fireplace's black funnel; this mouth was not square but narrow, a dark slit.

Then a very high, guttural, inhuman cry sounded from some mysterious place, from the well, from the stones of the house, from the soul of the kitchen's pots and pans, from the very breast of the young bride, who was shaken by it through and through. That bestial howl of agony soon proved to be a kind of joyous call: the man had burst through onto the roof. The muffled rubbings resumed more rapidly now; finally a black foot came down out of the slit searching for support—the foot of a hanged man. The foot found the first rung of the ladder and the young bride ran away.

In the courtyard, as the bride sat on a millstone, the old

housekeeper, one of those women for whom everything is new, assumed the task of keeping her informed; she walked back and forth bringing her the news with a mysterious air. "Now he is doing his cleaning under the hood," and the young bride pictured him as he shook off the soot, standing upright on the pile like a gravedigger on a mound of earth. "But what does he put on his feet to claw into the wall?" And then she ran after him to ask him: "My good man, what do you put on your feet to claw into the wall?" A gay reply followed which could not be heard clearly. "Now he is eating breakfast," and the housekeeper remained inside. Then she reappeared with a few small edelweiss; she said that the man had taken them out of a very clean little box and had offered them for the young bride.

After some time he himself came out, dressed again and with a pack on his back. He crossed the courtyard to leave, but the father stopped him and began to question him benevolently about his life. The young bride approached, too. Here the man, in the weak sun of winter, his face darker, his beard flecked with black and his eyes puckered by the light, looked like a big moth, a nocturnal bird surprised by the day. Or rather he looked like a spider or crab louse; the fact is that the hood of the hearth, when seen from below and if there is enough light outside, is not completely black but leaks a gray and slimy sheen.

He said that for thirty-five years he had been traveling through those towns cleaning the chimneys, that next year he would take his young son along to teach him the trade, that picking edelweiss was now forbidden and he had been able to gather those few flowers on the sly, and other such inconsequential things. Yet, whether astute or halting, it was quite clear that he only wished to hide himself behind those words, that he let the curtain of words fall in the same way that the cuttlefish beclouds the water.

He knew about all the deaths in the family, yet none of them had ever seen him!

By now the young bride felt that she was no longer ashamed for him, but was actually ashamed of herself.

After the chimney sweep had gone, she placed the few edelweiss beneath the portraits of the dead.

Translated by Raymond Rosenthal

The Death of the King of France

Clown admirable en vérité!

(Banville)

" ...CHINS up, lads. In five hours, at dawn, our fate will be decided. After the stirrup cup, the timid and disheartened can stay in the galley. But there won't be any of those, isn't that so? (Piercing and decisive glances into the eyes of all present.) Of course, we go forth and we do not know whether we'll return, but that's what makes life worth living! And if it is true that you have faith in me. . .I have not taught you anything, and it is not true that, as you often say, I am in any way your superior, but. . .(observing their reactions) but we have been comrades in a thousand glorious undertakings, and our destiny (satisfaction at his auditors' reactions) will not be a niggardly one, with our shinbones being used as pitchforks by those savages. Now go and try to sleep and dream of your women. You (noticing a motion made by the man he is addressing), yes, you, since you are on watch, wake me at four. And make sure, even if you have to douse me with a bucket of cold water. Is that clear? (Negligent sign of salute, two fingers touching forehead.) You, you and you stay here, for there's still something we have to discuss. (To all.) Just a moment, the orders for tomorrow." Intense semicircular glance: swift signs to call out the leaders one by one. Mutterings, stern looks in the eye, strong decisive gestures to each of them. Obviously, these are the assignments for the positions which must be held at all costs, and also the instructions on how to behave in all possible situations. Now his hands point to a mountain, now to a ravine, but without either his head or eyes moving to accompany the gesture. Then, to each man, a movement of the chin which means: "Back to your post"; and, almost at the same time, addressing one man or another with his outflung hand, (to a Chinaman in Chinese) "You understand? Nobody must go past that point!" (to an Italian in a southern dialect) "No noise, imagine that you are going to meet Peppe's wife at his house (sly smile) and don't smoke." (to a German in German) "Tomorrow morning, no beer drinking!" (Circular salute. The men have left. To two or three members of the general staff, in a southern Italian dialect and as if after heavy labor) "Well, let's hope for the best! It takes a lot out of you. . .(a bit tired) but that's the way you've got to talk to them. But the way I see it, it's going to be a dreadful mess tomorrow—that's the truth. Now then, let's take a look at. . .(Interrupted by knocks at the door. A crowd. Sound of yelling. But once again he is utterly authoritative and imperious.) What's going on here? What is it? (Still in dialect. Then:) What do you want, boy? Do you want to come with us? (Signs with hand, motioning men away from the back of the poop deck. Draws his large revolver with firm gesture and balances it, juggling it swiftly in his hand.) Now watch this. (Tosses up a large coin with left hand. A shot. The coin, hit, strikes against the rail and falls to the planking with a dull thud.) Now let's see you do it. And tell me, boy, do you have a mother? (Hands revolver to boy, barrel first.) It's your turn to show us something now. (Boy whirls about quickly. Simultaneous shot; the pipe is shattered between the teeth of the boatswain, who rubs his jaw, stunned. Sensation.) Excellent, by Christ! So you'll come with us." (All leave. Brief salute. Listens to something the man at his right is saying; does not approve but seems to be tempted. Lifts his eyebrows and lowers his head, as though to say: "Who knows? Maybe, perhaps. . ." Pretends absentmindedness. Reloads revolver with a jerk, thrusts it back into holster. Still in dialect.) "By God, I'm dead tired." (Gets up, making vague gesture. . . .)

The man who pronounced these words was an old and famous sea captain. To avoid inaccuracy, since it isn't quite certain whether his name was Smith, Dupont, Rossi, Mueller, Gonzales or Ivanov, we shall call him So-and-So. However, let this be clear right away, he was not inciting and readying his crew for a sortie against some fierce tribe living in the Sonda Islands, which had—let us say—captured an imprudent comrade. No, So-and-So had uttered the words related above only to himself, in the comfortable and friendly atmosphere of his toilet. during his laborious daily evacuation.

In this place, sacred to men's inner life and stimulating to their spirit, some have chosen to write their masterpieces, others to get over, by sublimating the most deep-seated feelings, the bitterness of amorous failure; but all persons double up on themselves to remember and meditate, and to try incessantly to understand the profound reasons of things and of their own souls. Thus So-and-So abandoned himself to memory and relived his heroic and mythical, adventurous and reckless life. Of course —let's be clear about this, too—he couldn't help but exaggerate a little. For, in that particular place, there sprang from his words and actions the image of an extraordinary So-and-So, not only polylingual and inured to all sorts of hardships, aware of all stratagems and emergencies, master of every situation and holder of the key to every eventuality (one of his specialties consisted in carrying to a conclusion the most unexpected and desperate enterprise by calling on elementary psychological motives or elementary physical laws which he manipulated with boundless deftness), but also wise in the most secret habits of beasts and men, in the most remote properties of vegetables and minerals of all latitudes, always smiling, and, like every respectable white hunter, with a smattering of scientific knowledge. If there was no fire, he produced it by mysterious rubbings; if there was no water, he extracted from the gum tree a "fresh and aromatic" liquid, and so on, and so on. Suppose that he found himself tied to a death stake with a mine beneath his feet and it was a question of putting out the already ignited fuse. Very well. While any-one else would have escaped by means of some sort of miraculous intervention or very complicated maneuver, which freed him from his bonds a split second before the fuse exploded the powder, So-and-So got out of the dangerous situation with a glob of spit directed with incredible precision, after having studied the direction of the wind and the specific weight of his saliva. Always wonderfully sure and calm, "endowed with exceptional self-possession and nerves of steel," infallibly skillful in handling weapons of every kind, furnished with very sharp senses and a perceptivity that grew apace in proportion to the danger, unusual physical stamina, capable of any physical and mental exploit and of bearing every wound and pain without batting an eye, perpetually invulnerable amid ambushes, perils, traps, hot lead and poisoned arrows, surrounded by a hand-picked phalanx of adventurers with famous names—Acrocerauni, De La Tour d'Auvergne (whom he addressed informally as Tour d'Auvergne)—all his precious collaborators. He not only—I say— seemed a physically perfect man and a perfect man of action, but also, may God forgive him, a scholar in many branches of knowledge, in glottology, history, an expert in law and mathematics—inevitably—and even inclined to literary debates, although at bottom he considered them the fritterings of women and the activity of weaklings. From the heights of his seat in the toilet he had, with his oral talents, amazed a committee of glottologists chosen from among the most learned in the world, had lectured on the ancient Chinese dynasties, and had granted audiences to all kinds of petitioners anxious to be enlightened on matters of the heart and the law.

Agreed, he boasted. For example, in his heart he knew very well that he did not know Chinese; and yet, in the above-mentioned speech, we have seen him speak to a sailor in this language. But imposture and mystification always contribute their share to the creation of all great men of action.

In general, one might say that the process of amplification and rounding out in the memory (secret pangs of conscience, shame?) ran parallel to another process, which the writer will call, provisionally, the decline of vocal potency. With the passing of the years, the speeches, lectures, and various stage appearances, at first declaimed in a loud voice and acted out with very statuesque poses, had little by little lost their vividness until they were only mumbled and hinted at and, in the end, withdrew somewhat further inside So-and-So's mind. To such an extent that now it would be hard to say whether the words were murmured or simply imagined, and whether the poses were merely unrealized thoughts. His voice and mimicry seemed to have retreated beneath the cover of his skin.

To bring this unpleasant subject of the toilet to an end, the writer must point out that whereas every man of true sensitivity naturally desires in his soul to be able to stay in there as long as possible, as in every other calm and comfortable place where we can best be ourselves—but because of real need: in fact the reasons for this great comfort are wholly physical and therefore the writer feels it unnecessary to mention them. Those who want to employ as little time as possible in satisfying that "vulgar" need are simply brutes. The chronically constipated are poor devils who have lost all freshness and candor; while those who are only partially and occasionally constipated are the happiest men in the world—this emotion was especially acute in So-and-So. He, by dint of desiring the beneficial bodily stimulus, in difficult or mixed-up or sad circumstances, or on the eve of some important decision, had reached the point of identifying sadness, indecisiveness, the need for clarification or consolation with that very stimulus. For obvious reasons this equation was irreversible. As a consequence, a disappointment could act only as a purge, but under no circumstances could the need act on him in the same way as, say, the discovery of his wife's adultery. On the other hand, how, during his adventurous and hazardous life, he had always succeeded in finding comfortable spots worthy of this description, is a mystery which the writer has never been able to solve.

In any event, an unacknowledged and malign weakness, which in itself could have placed him beside the giants and heroes of history and myth, would be enough to support the assertion—if there were still any need for this—that So-and-So was a great man of action. Like Achilles, like Samson and like Margutte, So-and-So had a weak spot. Spiders. Dread or religious horror, idiosyncrasy or abysmal attraction, the fact remains that So-and-So absolutely could not stand those tiny creatures. In ordinary speech one would say that "he was afraid of spiders." Entering a room where in the darkest, most remote corner nested the fragile, light-legged enemy, So-and-So detected it at once. If someone was with him he would beg him to catch it and throw it away, but without hurting it;[1] otherwise,

---

[1] How indeed can one tolerate the sight of an innocent spider which, crushed by some clumsy broom, still attempts to flee, strewing the floor with its legs and smearing it with a yellowish slime (its blood!), tottering wildly on its few remaining legs and then, finally, lying with its legs cross-shaped, dead?

staking his all—as he himself would say at such moments—he
armed himself with the longest possible pole and began a so-to-
speak hand to hand struggle with the enemy, slashing out with
great cleaving, thwacking strokes. Once, when So-and-So was
still a young boy and was exploring his large house at night—it
is not quite clear under what circumstances—suddenly, beneath
the steps of a wooden stairway which led to the attic, there it was:
a huge gelatinous spider of a fleshy yellow color. At first dismayed, then perhaps heartened by the realization that he was
indeed walking through the house at night, So-and-So thought
that it would be appropriate to touch the spider with the flame
of the candle and burn it: the spider gave a prodigious bound
and vanished in the air. Well, our hero, who of course was walking about in his nightshirt with bare legs, was seized by such
a dreadful frenzy because of the fear that the spider might have
fallen on him that, for an indefinite time, he kept hopping
convulsively from one foot to the other. Time passed, but whenever So-and-So happened to go up that stairway he shied like a
colt. On another occasion a spider crept over So-and-So's neck as
he was sleeping and when he saw it later on the bed, he moved
lock, stock and barrel to another room to sleep, or perhaps to stay
awake, assailed by unspeakable nightmares. For a long time he
had feared that the touch of a spider would be enough to stop
his heart forever, but after that episode he used to mutter: "Yes,
we have a pretty tough hide!"

It would take too long to relate all the details of So-and-So's
stormy relations with spiders. In any case, it is still a matter
for wonder that during the course of the life described above,
the captain succeeded in victoriously resisting the assaults of the

inevitable, monstrous, tropical spiders; besides, his enemies would have required only a handful of spiders to disrupt his whole lofty strategy, and that handful would have produced a much more sensational effect than all of Pyrrhus' elephants.

Such was the man who, having stood up and performed all the other customary formalities, prepared to issue from the toilet. And right away a feeling of irritation overcame him: in fact, after having opened and shut the door, he had to undertake a thorough cleansing of his fingers, dirtied by contact with the doorknob. That knob was not especially dirty, but it was nevertheless the knob "of the toilet." Just as when out walking So-and-So had to press all protruding cobblestones exactly with the center of his sole, so he could not bear the contact of dirty things. If it were a question of tactile contamination, cleansing was achieved by an opportune spit on the tip of one finger, which then moistened the other fingertips and the infected portion of the palm. If, however, the dirty object had simply been seen, or a scatalogical expression had been heard, the ceremony consisted in expelling by force the exhalations which had clung to the eyes and ears. As for these snorts from the mouth—kisses blown into the air in memory of the dear departed—all this exigent and painstaking ritual, other writers have already dealt with them and there is no point in repeating it here.

Therefore, So-and-So spat into his palm, rubbed his hands and, finally, having seen to all his inner needs, turned with a benevolent look to life.

It was understandable that he should do so; it was a crystalline day at the very beginning of spring, with a bright sun shining and everything clear, fresh, etched. So-and-So crossed the courtyard full of burgeoning greenery; and then, from the door of the living room, Rosalba came to meet him.

2

Louange aux femmes pour leur vie merveilleuse!

The sun had barely begun its heavenly passage. Rosalba was a little girl of perhaps twelve or thirteen years of age. Wearing a robe, ready for her bath. "I'm ready, papa," she in fact cried, as soon as she saw So-and-So. Indeed, it ought to be known that besides a sickly, yellow-eyed little son, left him by his deceased wife, So-and-So also had this Rosalba, who had been adopted at a tender age "to give a little sister to the baby boy," and who believed that he was her father. With her help he hoped to carry out an old plan which had become possible only now that, as he said, he had retired from business (and by business he meant that astonishing life of his). The plan was to watch over and accompany the growth and flowering of a female body. (In fact he would add—"and of a soul"—but the writer takes the liberty of doubting this last assertion.) To achieve this, it had been necessary to raise the small creature along special lines, that is, banning *a priori* certain conventions and feelings of shame, avoiding dangerous contacts, etc. This was actually what So-and-So had taken pains to do and—one must admit— with the best of results. Thus, for example, he had accustomed his charge to take her daily bath in his presence: in this way he had the opportunity to observe day by day the development and changes in that frail body. What he expected from such observations or in the long run, that is, when her development had been fulfilled, and what he got out of it, the writer cannot imagine. But just as a mere suggestion, the writer will venture the hypothesis that it was not a matter of pure esthetic interest and that So-and-So would not have subjected himself to the trouble of watching a young girl's bath every blessed day, if he did not have in prospect the moment when this child would begin to be a woman: in short, if he were not interested in seeing the fruit slowly ripen. But there was perhaps something more in that desire for close contact with the intimate details of a young girl's life, something more subtle.

In any case, up till now everything had gone according to plan. And Rosalba (this could be seen when, with a naïve gesture, she let her robe fall to the floor of the bathroom) had become a superb young girl. With great, deep eyes, her short hair soft and shining. Perhaps a trifle thin. The bathroom was simply a kind of closet rearranged for the purpose, and the door was always flung open to let in the light: the first tepid rays of the sun, together with the trees and bushes two paces beyond the threshold, cast bluish reflections on her frail, already blooming body. That body was neither milky nor virginal (white is the brazen hue of modesty), but rather brownish, beyond virginity and sin. Because of its muted tone, the curve of her loins made one think of the sound of a flute. Her legs had grown a bit thicker and sturdy, to support a slight torso, her shoulders were slanted and a bit bent, so that her breasts, drooping somewhat, lapped against the light, nearly transparent skin over her ribs, while her belly was ample and concave, shaded by brown and purple and with blonde tints in the upper part, almost like sprouting vegetation. Pointed hips (they were the feature which immediately struck one about her). That body, as though still benumbed by the warmth of bed, filled with drowsiness and shivering in the cool air, blossomed without shame, leaning slightly to one side, like the body of one of those Madonnas carved from an elephant's tusk. Without shame: Rosalba regarded her bath in her father's presence and all her intimacies with him as an ordinary, habitual thing, and perhaps did not even suspect that other girls, especially those of her age, do not as a rule undress in front of their fathers. The absence of shame was precisely the circumstance which made it possible for So-and-So to realize his plan. He was therefore extremely careful not to arouse her hidden sensitivity. Holding his breath every instant, tense from the effort of not betraying himself, whether he entered her room as she was slipping on her thin underwear, or helped her to sponge the least accessible parts of her body, he always had to disguise vigilantly whatever carnal feeling might exist in his solicitude and give himself a natural, unconcerned aspect; if he had behaved otherwise, it would have furthered her unconscious formative process. In this inflexible surveillance of himself at each and every moment, lay perhaps So-and-So's keenest, most complete pleasure. Even admitting this, and even admitting his awareness that each decisive intimacy might at bottom signify the destruction of that voluptuous familiarity, one must still ask where the devil he found the strength to resist the spell of that young body, especially now that the natural solution was on the point of frustrating all his watchfulness.

Perhaps one must also admit that the naturalness of his relations with the girl was not at all feigned, and that precisely in this was hidden the situation's voluptuousness. Put another way, he was sure of having the girl in his power, wholly and for any purpose. It is enough to conceive a feeling of assurance for it to pass into a remote region of our soul, where it ends by becoming impersonal and generic, that is, beyond the particular object which gave rise to it. There are many people for whom it is enough to be able to do a thing for them no longer to have a need to do it, and to feel satisfied, as if they actually had done it. But all these explanations are not really necessary.

After her bath, Rosalba is now ready to begin her day. And at this point the writer would like to have at his disposal a palette covered with subdued crystalline colors, shining yet diaphanous. Of what is the day of a twelve or thirteen-year-old girl composed? No doubt of small, nameless events, laughter beneath the light gold of her lashes—as a woman poet of some distant land has sung. Unfortunately the writer does not possess either the mythical naïveté or the pure vigor of that poetess and therefore he will renounce, to his dishonor and regret, the describing of that laughter. The sun, however, continued its heavenly passage, described an even loftier arc, reached its peak, remained for an instant as if suspended, and then sadly began its descent toward the horizon; but let us not be troubled, for tomorrow it will rise again, tomorrow it will be the same old story.

But with the falling of the sun the evening approaches and, with the evening, the shadows, the carriers of voluptuous terrors. But not only the shadows, the friends, too; the friends who gather each evening in So-and-So's house. So-and-So was well aware that these encounters could be dangerous for Rosalba (and in fact, while recounting his prodigious adventures, he did not lose sight of her for a moment): yet he had permitted them to take place out of inertia or necessity, or perhaps because he also feared solitude as the worst of all the dangers facing his ward.

For this task—namely, to describe such desolate and exciting small-town family gatherings—one needs instead the somber colors which are surely available to certain great prose writers of our time. In his inadequacy, the writer sees himself compelled to pass up another fine opportunity and, although his position threatens to become untenable, to decline this chore as well.

To these gatherings came a lawyer, indeed *the* lawyer, with his twenty-eight-year-old son (black mustaches), the pharmacist, the local magistrate, and who else? Well, the mayor, the councilmen and various officials with their respective wives; and, whether they listened in a semicircle to accounts of So-and-So's crocodile hunts or, let us say, the phonograph, whether they tripped about to the ritual dance tunes or played the most decrepit parlor games, they always enjoyed themselves quite properly and respectably.

> Creola
> Dalla bruna aureola
> Per pietà sorridimi
> Che l'amor m'assal.

But that evening Rosalba—it is hard to say why—became inexplicably irritated during a game of "wireless" by the whisperings of the person next to her (the drooling magistrate), and walked out on the terrace to get some air. Strange! the sensation of that warm breath persisted on her ear and cheek and that murmur, which had been hissed out with a chesty effort and had moreover been incomprehensible, still buzzed within her and gave no sign of going away—both the breath and the murmur seemed to be endowed with all the attributes of a gross physical presence. After a while, curiously enough, the lawyer's son came after her. But So-and-So had noticed the maneuver and managed to find a pretext to join them. Coming out, he saw them close together beneath a tuft of greenery: the young man was talking rapidly and Rosalba was caught full in the face by a sodden moon: her eyes were darkened by it. The girl listened, her eyebrows slightly raised and her delicate mouth pursed in a heart-shape, as small children do. An impalpable breath seemed to come from that mouth, a sharp odor of verbena (that clod who was talking to her obviously felt it); and the moon thrust a keen, cold blade between her teeth into the dark hollow of her mouth.

Then all the guests left, lingering for a long time in the hallway, saying good-bye, in those very last moments recovering all their wit, and like new-fledged phoenixes, from their yawning languor the most vital subjects were reborn: "So, it seems that they're going to add another trip to the bus schedule. . . ."

And so to bed.

3

In solchen Naechten waechst mein Schwesterlein...

(Rilke)

But that night Rosalba could not sleep. She couldn't because there were too many problems to solve. For some time now
there had been an obscure menace in all things. First of all,
what did those moist and sticky looks of the lawyer's mustachioed son mean, when he called in the evening? Looks
drowned in a force greater than himself and thus imploring,
not imperious, not insistent. And what did it mean that her
father now sometimes gnawed at his lips, or turned away his
glance as from an unhappy sight, during her baths? And now
he almost never gave her any advice, nor did he help her—the
curve of her loins frequently remained untouched by the sponge.

It was that which one had to discover. And then, that dis-
consolate weeping over the sunsets and the old house, when she
saw it, from some far corner of the garden, livid in the late sunset, that weeping over the buds and the green of the trees, that
inner weeping which produced tears which were rare but big
and slow and heavy, when she felt them run down her cheeks,
tears which were pried loose with difficulty from the calm
eye socket. . . . It is perhaps right that a sunset should cause tears,
certainly, but one must absolutely know why this happens,
owing to which precise element. In order to be able to conclude:

Yes, that's it, I understand, it's the red that upsets me!—But no, one weeps and one does not know why, there is a tranquil threat in everything; or rather, a widening of one's eyes as of children before something sad and unfamiliar—like the dead, swollen with sorrow, staring down from their portraits in the chapels. And worse yet, the sponge's coarseness is now almost pleasant and thrilling on the arch of her loins, her breath is heavy with a weight that forces her to heave a sigh every five minutes. That's it, yes, perhaps that's it—one is sad not because one is sad but because, when one sighs, one's soul must find a reason for that sighing. In any case, at the bottom of that weight lies the promise of a new, hidden pleasure. A pleasure: but what, may I ask? Perhaps it is necessary to free oneself from that weight with a deeper, deeper sigh, an unimaginable sigh—it is only a moment, one ascends, ascends even more inside, even deeper, to the point of vertigo, to the point of snatching the ultimate tuft of breath which is knotted up in the depths (but the depths of what?) and then one is freed. But perhaps not: perhaps that weight must increase indefinitely without respite, until the blood erupts in a furious roar, beating, beating at the temples, the throat, the wrists, the armpits, the sounding fingertips. It is necessary that the weight be crushed, yes *crushed*.

Tonight all the noises do not sleep, do not die out after their desperate appeal, and every near and far-off sound dances a dangerous saraband. A threatening one. The shrill grinding of a wagon on the distant moonlit road grows and swells with the same rhythm as the blood in her head—a terrible rhythm, not fast, but pressing, mounting—it swells with an obscure and frightening menace: wa-gon, wa-gon. It swells, it is just about to burst wide open. Oh Lord, this time it did not burst, this time it passed by and is collapsing like a breaker. But the next wave, what will it be, what will it be? It is indeed a sea with huge stormy blades and among the blades a huge, square-headed monster with the body of a snake. The monster tries to reach out with its dreadful head, but the backwash pulls it away. But the wash also brings it closer, and, in time with the beating of the waves, every so often (at each surge!) the monster rears up, shrieks, rears up on the incoming breaker, and as it rears up it shrieks with an all-encompassing, deafening voice, and when it is at the highest point, when its head has covered the horizon and its body the sea, precisely then its shriek reaches its intensest pitch and completely fills the air. There is no escape: the air is a shriek, the sea is a body, the horizon is its head. The breaker topples over and the monster with it; yet again the breaker surges up and this time, who can tell? perhaps this time the monster will seize its prey. It has not seized it; the monster has been grazed by its breath, but there are still as many breakers as there are seconds in eternity. . . One more leap, but again it slithers down, then again it leaps up to seize us. . .but it cannot: the waves are as numerous as the pulse-beats of time, but they are not all breakers and if the wash does not push forward the monster's leap, how will it be able to catch up with us? The breakers are calmed, the sea is calmed, grumbling the monster leaves. There is a clap of thunder. It is over. But now the tranquil sea is pitch, the sky is lead, monstrous, tawny shrimp graze us with their long feelers, their eyes hornlike and hard, pitiless eyes. Yet their spiteful slowness is so marmoreal that they will not have us. Oh Lord, when will the sun shine again over the sea,

when will the water be as radiant as flowing gold? *Flowing*:
that is the answer—*flowing, crushed*. Oh look, at last a little sun.
All you have to do is repeat any word, turning it over in your
head, for it to be emptied of its everyday meaning. It's funny,
really funny. That's not all: *binoculars*: I don't know where it
comes from, but *binoculars*! It's not beautiful, just funny.
Laughing laughing! Bottles, champagne, women, the lawyer's
son. . . .

But the laughter is macabre; wait, it comes from the small
alcove at the top of the stairs, the alcove enclosed by the three
walls of the old courtyard. Or is it us? Is it I? Why yes, I am
floating in the air and looking at that laughter. Floating in the
air, but now we dive into an enormous funnel of air and lead.
Only the laughter. Farewell, flights over the Serra Capriola,
farewell, free fluttering of arms over the mountain valleys! No
more, gentlemen, we are falling! The laughter again. That is,
it was there. And now? We search for this blessed laughter,
macabre of course but at bottom quite friendly, which amuses
itself by running away through the closed door like a will-'o-the-
wisp. The house! It is in the house. But the other house is off our
path. The other house! What does it mean? It means that we
cross the rooms in between, those clustered around the inside
staircase, but we do not search through all the halls on the second
floor. No, obviously we must descend the wooden, winding
stairway that leads to the kitchen. Downstairs it is best to look
first into the pantry on the right; in fact it is certain that the
laughter has taken refuge there. Silly thing, it may be behind
the greasy door, which doesn't open all the way and leaves a
space next to the wall. It must be behind the door and perhaps

once it is discovered it will shout "ha-ha," gaily. The pantry. No, there is no laughter here. Oh, what a bore—where did it go? Perhaps it is still off to the right, perhaps it went through the lumber room and is out in the courtyard again. Of course. But why doesn't it rest a while? Here's the wooden bushel, so let's sit down. Oh, how clear everything is, mercifully distinct and gray-colored! How distinctly one sees everything! Behind my back the game pouch, I don't even have to turn to know it is there; beyond the fly screen, a piece of salted cheese, thick blue spaghetti paper (and what is *that* doing here?) and . . .but what is that? Oh, it's a partridge. In the corner the skewers, on this side the pots, a row of pots arranged by size on a shelf, on the other side the pot covers held up against the wall with a wire, also in order of size. The mouth of the cistern. The coil of the chain hanging on a nail, a basket filled with leaves and three plates (but why, I should like to know, is it called the pantry!) and across the way stands the sink, though of course the water isn't running: they wash the dishes there and there's a hole for the water to flow away, that's why they call it a sink. What else? Dark yellow, dirty, worm-eaten beams. A bacon rind. Ha-ha, the rind. But there is absolutely nothing to say about the rind. Rind, and that's all. *Rind*: this is funny too. Potatoes on the floor! Sprouting. Potatoes, as we know, are animals. They lift a strange head with a long neck from their warty bodies. The neck and head green, the body earth-colored. Strange animals. Too fresh a head for that decrepit body. Like. . .like what? Come, what a silly idea. . .but after all, from the body of dogs there sometimes sprouts a thin pinkish flesh, retractile and sensitive as the horns of a snail. Yes. . .dogs are strange animals too. But

how frightening all this is! In any case, let us call the potatoes. . .
"dogesses." Now there's a pretty word: "Peel the dogesses and
slice them thin." Sounds good. Surely there is something mysterious in these tender potato heads, that is, these dogesses.
Mysterious—it is no longer something to be laughed or joked
about, not even something to be talked about to oneself. One
must withdraw to the darkest depths of one's soul to study, no,
to hope to be penetrated by the revelation. The revelation of the
tender heads. My goodness, we're no longer gay. Dismay is all
that's left. Numbness, sadness. But let's try the usual system:
hole. No, *hole* doesn't work—a hole is a hole. But why did I
say hole? Ah yes, because right in front of me there is a large
hole, not the hole in the sink but the one in the floor, in the gray
concrete pavement stained with greasy water—a hole for the
water to drain down and flow away.

Now everything disappears. The black hole cannot be seen
anymore. It fills the horizon all by itself, just like the sea monster. But it does not shriek, it keeps silent. It really isn't ac-
curate to say that it fills the horizon: those are just words. It is
still there, at the usual distance, on the edge of the gray, grease-
stained concrete floor. But suppose a strange beast, a beast
never seen before, suddenly rose out of that hole! Oh my goodness! starting from that hole the beast could wander all over the
house, cautiously, softly slither in everywhere, nestle under the
pillows, huddle in the armpits of those who are sleeping—oh
why didn't I think of this before! And what has love got to do
with it? *Love*: here too it doesn't work. *Hole* and *love* are
refractory.

And then Rosalba stiffens with horror. Horror does not

close her eyes, it holds them wide open and rigid, shining and immobile like gray pools. Rosalba's eyes take in the entire universe, and at the center of the universe there is the black hole. Out of the black hole something is pushing with a certain effort, though with the soft suppleness of cats when they slip through a door that is slightly ajar. A gray, slimy form sticks out its head, its neck, its body. Yet, though it is so gray and slimy that it cannot be distinguished against the floor and wall, gradually, as it advances, one can discern its head, neck and body. But what am I saying, "discern"! The truth is, one can see or sense that the form has a head, a neck, a body. Anyway (and if the description isn't clear, it doesn't matter) it is a beast. In fact it is *the* beast. One of those things which, animate or not, strike us like a bolt of lightning, one of those things which fill us with careful, meticulous horror, one of those enormous, unspeakable things, and it isn't true that one can observe all of its minute particulars.[2] Exactly how the beast is formed cannot be said. However, it has hard, corneous, clotted eyes, like those of animals that do not see, opaque and veiled like the eyes of walruses. A soft, viscid muzzle, very long, thin, sensitive whiskers shivering at the air's touch. Observing it more closely one can see that the muzzle shivers more than a rabbit's, indeed all the skin of its face shivers. There is no other way of describing it because the beast's head, rearing erect on its high neck where the slime was

---

[2] Correct! interjects the writer, as always inappropriately. Does one remember the color of the eyes of a dead woman one has loved? Rather than reality, it is the fantastic form which in such circumstances takes shape in us, and this, since it is fantastic, does not have logical attributes but only ideal ones.

marked by furrows, had something human about it. Its eyes looked straight ahead, not to the side or shiftily. Its body. . .its body, well, it's hard to say. But it was easy to sense its general shape. The beast was a head, like certain men are a nose. A monstrous head, delicate and sensitive like. . .I've found it! . . . like the head of the dogesses! The blind beast was tensely stretched forward. Toward what? Oh, from the very first moment Rosalba understood that it was stretched toward her. There is nothing we understand better than the intentions of our kin (and why not call it one of our kin?) when they are completely unexpressed. If someone says "I want to kill you," perhaps he is implying something else, but if someone wants to kill us and does not say so, how quickly we understand it!

Tensed and hard but not hurrying, the beast advanced with the calm of beings sure of themselves. The livid eyes had no look in them, yet were greedily fixed on their prey. Eyes whose power could not be escaped: eyes which had no expression and were not human. Blind eyes in the service of an inflexible, secret light. Slow and sure, the beast came. But if it was blind, it did not see with its eyes. Then how could one try to escape them? It would be the same as wanting to escape from a lion simply because it is blind, while one feels continually seen and hounded by its sense of smell. So one must endure, endure it, but oh my God, let the torment be brief! We stand stockstill, yet may it come and catch us if we are in its power! The beast, however, is taking its time. There is plenty of time to look into the hard, hornlike eyes, the eyes which do not move; yes, they can be looked at, Rosalba can look at them at her ease. No more terror now—a peaceful, pursuing stare. So this is the beast which can wander all over the house and enter everywhere, nestle under a sleeper's pillow, in the hollow of one's armpits, between one's . . .yes, between one's warm thighs. Poor beast which lives in the holes of sinks in a perpetual wetness, greasy with dirty water, it wishes the warmth. Oh, is that a pain. . .between the thighs? No. An itch? No, it is a fire and a sharp tightening, as though by tightening but one nerve, all the body's nerves responded. That was before, but now one must fill this fixity, one cannot await the first contact of the beast's head with a blank mind. *Love*: no, that doesn't work. It's useless. We've seen that already. But now let's try something else. "The dog suffers if his master eats and does not give him anything" (one of papa's sayings). Yes, this is the truth. All people feed their dogs when they eat themselves. At last, a sure standard. One knows exactly what to think of the sadness of dogs when they watch us eat and can't manage to get anything—simply because the meaning of this sadness has been clearly expressed, once and for all. But other things which only we can discover, even though more satisfying, are not at all satisfying and never certain. Thus, perhaps more pleasant.[3] Anyway, how does all this fit in? It comes in because of love. . .therefore its meaning is never certain.

There's no point in trying to make head or tail of such reasoning—these thoughts have now that accelerated, false rhythm when the mind does not follow them, because it is else-where, fragmented among the appearances of things. Then the

[3]In short, Rosalba is alluding, perhaps unconsciously, to the re-assuring certainty of the so-called apodictic truths. Perhaps she was trying to hint at the existence of a category of events beyond ex-perience: events which cannot be known.

mind is not a mind, it is utterly molten and flowing (and it takes on the color of fire)—farther down, farther up, who knows where? to the mouth of the stomach, to the roots of the hair, prickling. This is the true mind. It is fear, no, not fear at all: fixity. Prick-ling, prick-ling, preeck.

Preeck—but the beast has not understood anything of all this. Silent, it is now a handsbreadth from Rosalba, on the floor: it reaches no higher than halfway up her shin. It wants her legs to open slowly. So let's slowly open the legs. It doesn't want her to be wearing a nightgown or anything. But she didn't have one on. Come to think of it, the iron rim of the bushel feels cold on her behind. So: Rosalba is seated on the bushel, her legs tenderly open. The beast is on the floor, a handsbreadth from her body, between her legs. And now, with the unerringness of a goat which instantly chooses the softest cluster of grapes, the beast, with a small silent leap, takes possession of Rosalba. It lunges to bite off her most tender bud, which its blind sense of smell had immediately revealed to it: Should she struggle? She knows that is impossible. The bush-el is cold, the bush-el is co-o-old (to the tune of "Bandolino stanco"). Softness with softness, that's how it should be. But the beast hasn't torn off anything, it hasn't torn off her most tender bud, there in the crevice of her thighs, in order to eat it. The beast wants to suck her all over. Very well, let it. Pain? But what are you saying, milady? No, there's not the slightest pain. The beast simply hangs there, sucking. Let it suck, there's no pain. Rosalba merely gazes at a little pottery vase, so pretty with its arms on its hips. And when is the pain going to come? Perhaps it isn't ever supposed to come. Poor little beast, blind and dreadful, gray and slimy, what are you doing? But I don't mind—go on, go on. But now, suddenly, this seriousness. There's no point, though, in fighting against this either. Pain, pain? No, joy. No, not that either, but the small vase begins to move, making a wide circle, a circle so wide that if it goes on like that it will certainly be carried way out behind the stars. Good-bye, lovely little vase. And the cement floor and the sink and the walls and the dirty yellow beams, first in a whirl, then pulling back, all vanish. Look: on that pearly gray, the color of the void, the rind floats again. Silence. Yet nothing is left and that nothing is flecked by a silent uprush of lymph, by a pouring of emptiness into emptiness, by hyacinth skies pouring into skies, by peach-colored universes pouring into universes. Silence and an earsplitting noise.

And now the uprush of jadelike lymph becomes clearer. It does not bubble up, it flees. It flows irremediably and softly, it purifies, liberates, carries off life (life?), everything. The blood, the veins, the bones and bowels dissolve and flow away in lymph. Purification, liberation! Liberation and perhaps— yes, yes—life! The lymph melts, flows.

It flows. Neither sadness nor joy, because neither of these is truly necessary. Necessary (because it is) is the melting of the lymph, the flowing. It flows and the beast is no longer there and Rosalba is once again alone, this time standing on the gray cement floor, naked and white with the purple shadow of her belly, and, lower down, her triangular shadow. But what about life? And now (perhaps some lymph rising up again?) now something pulling, at first faint, then sharp, inside, down there. But what, what is it? Blood, yes blood. A peaceful stream of blood which flows down from the purple hollow, flows and spreads and weaves a triangular film, transparent as a cascade. But if it is peaceful, there's no need to be alarmed. Yet, yet. . . the blood is filling the entire room, the triangle narrows, narrows, disappearing in the rising lake with a calm, soft submergence of sound. Rosalba looks at herself—soon the triangle will be gone and the blood will have reached her hips. Oh, to be able to get up, to run away. Run away? The blood is a soothing, lovely bath. It is not hot, but cool. Liberation—it flows. But it keeps rising, that's what's wrong. A spasm in the entrails, the loins. And now, here beneath her chin, two slight but heavy globes of flesh with tender points like those of the dogesses. Spasm.

And Rosalba wakes up with a start. As in a train, she abruptly resumes contact with reality. Reality is a warm dripping between her thighs. A jerk of the hand and her blanket is thrown off: blood, really blood. Broad bloodstains on the sheet. And still a hidden tingling of warm blood. Warm, not cool, black. Instinctively Rosalba leaps to her feet. She wants to call her papa, but something holds her back.

Perhaps the reader does not know what "flowing" means. Perhaps he is unaware of the precise conditions under which the obscure force which compels a drop to fall, if nothing holds it back, unfolds in all its crystalline clarity. As always, a vaster law here expresses itself through the particular law. There exist a pure and an impure flowing. From no part of a man can something flow purely: a drop of mucous which drips from his nose will inevitably follow a broken line, that is, it must slide along an inclined surface before attaining its divine, arrowlike verticality, aimed at the heart of the earth. In him a pure flow can occur only from peripheral organs; something which starts from within, from his most profound substance, can never flow out of him purely (thus perhaps, man, to his misfortune, is not subject to monthly cathartic cleansings). At the most one can imagine a diffusion of blood from the tips of his fingers held open along his thighs. So let us hope that on some distant day a halo of flowing threads of blood may enmesh our legs: this is our dream.

But for a woman it is another matter. From a woman, from her innermost precordia, the blood can flow logically and with stellar purity. Indeed, each thick, heavy drop of fearful blood which strikes the floor with a neat, dull sound is the direct projection of that woman's center of gravity and it traces its ideal trajectory through the air. And if, drop falling on drop, there forms a tranquil, mercurial lake of lazy, convex, thick liquid with shining borders, the bewildered siren arising from that lake will be Rosalba herself, the center and fulcrum of that tide.

Apparently calm, Rosalba contemplated that little lake, though a subtle thought kept nagging at the walls of her soul, like a horsefly in the spring. So this is love—the girl said to herself. And if she simply believed she knew, what else matters? It is enough to believe that one sees to see—insofar as it is true that nothing exists. And at this point the writer must beg the reader's pardon for having yielded, for the sake of fidelity, to an excessive accuracy in depicting Rosalba's state of being.

4

She has gone to others, the insomnia-nurse

(Akhmatova)

Certainly spring had come to maturity in a single night, and summer arrived bearing in its hands sheaves of frenzy and the insomnia-nurse: for that night So-and-So had also felt a boundless oppression and thirst. If that heavy semidrowsiness could have been incarnated in a thought and image, it would doubtlessly have been that of his ward Rosalba who, from behind a brilliant, purplish mist, like a naked swimmer seen from the bottom of the sea, flashed between his eyelids. A stroke of the arm and the sea's bottom recedes, first slowly, then more swiftly, and in a moment our arms can embrace both the water's surface and the swimming girl. So-and-So sat up; he was already awake.

So-and-So knew that the two mouths seen so unknowingly close together in the dim lunar light would one day be united, paradisiacally or terrestrially (but he did not know that the major of the grenadiers had already smeared his ward's virginal lips with an unreciprocated kiss; he did not know that that drool would froth and ferment around the curve of her mouth). Which is to say that one day Rosalba would refuse to take her daily bath in his presence, or would take it blushing and with effort, or simply because he ordered her to, thus ending his felicitous indecision and forcing him to assume a clear-cut attitude toward her.

He had known this, but had always pushed away the thought with dread. But now the imminence of that moment seemed to him—who knows why?—strangely present and he felt that he must immediately concern himself with it.

Oppression, thirst. . .and now, at last, a specific desire: to drink. So-and-So got up cautiously; his little son was sleeping in the next room, and he was such a nervous, fragile child that interrupting his sleep would be unforgivable. Without knowing quite how, he found himself in front of the mirror and, with an habitual gesture, stuck out his coated tongue. Seen from the corner of his eye, the open scissors on the chest of drawers looked like a big spider which had lost four of its legs in a battle. Yet So-and-So, already accustomed to this arachnomorphosis, was not startled. The hairs on his chest inside the neck of his light pajamas were graying; gray hairs, and so abundant, were also on his temples; wrinkles on his brow, at the corners of his eyes—crow's-feet, the women call them. "You'll soon be sixty, old boy!" And, almost naturally, he repeated a very old gesture which he thought he had buried forever: he uncovered himself. Torso: gray hairs, his breasts marked by a billow of fat and the usual, ridiculous race of neatly arranged hairs down to his navel. He uncovered himself further: lower down the nearly pointed swelling out of his belly, traversed by that neat race of hairs (Mountain Climber's Day; that one there, forging ahead of all of them, darker, isn't he the Flea of the Pyrenees?). Farther down, flabby flesh, grown inescapably flabby, and gray there too. That's what's serious about it! "Well, it's nothing new, and who gives a good God damn," he said, perhaps aloud, and covered himself. The bath, the bath: how could he continue to preserve the girl's incredible unawareness? Yes, her curves are filling out, it is inevitable that she will go through the white world like a butterfly.[4] There's nothing to be done. What had he been thinking about? Oh yes, a glass of water. So-and-So noiselessly opened the door. Now he had to cross the boy's room: the child was sleeping and from his half-opened lips, his sweat-beaded forehead, fumed something feverish and morbid. Just look at him, So-and-So said to himself, walking past the bed without touching it (his thoughts had quickly taken another turn)—it's lucky that he has his eyes closed. Some father I am, by God, I haven't even managed to decide what color his eyes are!—but here too, there was nothing to be done, he had studied it for a long time and had never succeeded in getting anywhere. Yet, considering the matter carefully, when he had to compare the color of those eyes with that of other known objects, So-and-So felt his whole being revolt, as though seized by terror. His reason and memory refused to function properly, as if they feared every deeper probe might produce a frightful revelation. That's just what happened now, and So-and-So, who had finally reached the door of the kitchen, managed to distract himself from this thought. His sharp desire for water maintained his balance: a frail desire, somewhat like the pine branch one clings to while crawling from one mountain ledge to another above a gorge in which a boraciferous fumarole or a bubbling of sulphurous waters fills the air with fire and smoke. At last, the water; two green glass bottles which had survived all cataclysms, such as are often

---

[4]The writer must again beg pardon for the dubious imagery of our excellent captain, who obviously also had read Russian novels.

used to preserve tomatoes. They stand in the copper basin, cool. Now, where is a glass? No, better to drink straight from the bottle. His thirst is momentarily quenched. So the balance is upset. So-and-So himself is aware of it, for he feels that again he is dangling above the fumarole and tries to fool himself into thinking that he is still thirsty. Oh, thank God, a fleabite. These abominable fleas, you can't remain a minute with bared legs without their attacking you and trying to suck out your soul! There are plenty of them and everywhere in this house. Is it the dog? (Anyway, this is good, we can think about the fleas.) The itch becomes stronger, stable and stinging. It's a nuisance to catch the flea and crush it at once between your fingertips— otherwise, as soon as it touches the floor and before you know it, it bounds away and vanishes. Then you have to wash your fingers. Oh, what a bore! Alas, you have to.

And So-and-So bent over resentfully to catch the flea— ah there it is, on the anklebone (he was only wearing slippers and pajamas). Caught and already stunned, rolled between thumb and index finger, all I can do now is let it fall and then let's hope I can see it on this gray, wrinkly floor. The flea falls, but something gray, diaphanous and impalpable as a shadow, something threadlike and tenuous, as though borne by the air, enters So-and-So's field of vision. He was not quite sure that he had seen it, like those things which barely flash by at the extreme bounds of our vision and which (illusion, reality?) we bring back into focus with a certain amazement; yet his heart—the heart which is never wrong—had already warned him of the danger and seemed to freeze in his breast. In that corner of the large kitchen the light of the tipsy bulb fought against the shadow which, along the wall, encircled and swallowed it. The yellowish, already feeble light thinned out on the gray floor and grew gray itself. Little more than a shadow. It was the middle of the night and a stonelike silence bore down, an impenetrable silence with stern, tight-drawn lips. In that light and silence, a spider, neither large nor small due to that diaphanous grayness, was crawling across the kitchen.

It was a spider of the most common species, of a family without a name, the kind with very long, thin legs, like hairs, and with a pepper-grain body. It proceeded jauntily, according to its custom, but without haste: without the least creak it hobbled along on its impossible legs, which seemed to adhere stickily to the floor, pulling them in with small tugs which should have seriously upset its equilibrium if many other legs of the same sort hadn't immediately re-established it on the other side. The minute grain of its body, as if in the throes of an astral storm, tottered wildly on the airy pattern of its supports and, from time to time, when the shadow overflowed and devoured the pattern, seemed to float on the mere air in a monstrously rhythmic saraband. That's how it went forward, and yet in that being there was something silent and solemn, like the advance of destiny, something which we clearly discern during our sleepless nights. So-and-So, though his legs were bare and the spider passed two feet from his face (the most intimate point of the body), did not begin jumping frenetically, as on that other occasion. He didn't even try to move. Perhaps because he hadn't foreseen the danger in time and suddenly found himself too close, he didn't alter his position in the slightest and, struck to the heart, remained just like that, bent over, fascinated and immobile. The flea, everything in the world apart from the floor and the spider, were outside his perception. Under normal conditions a certain exasperated, clearly tactile sensitivity in his fingertips would have told him that he had not yet cleansed them of the filthy contact with the flea. But the feeling had vanished just as it was about to declare itself.

That other being, the spider, was also following a precise direction: So-and-So knew instantly that its implacable course would bring it to pass an inch, perhaps less, from the tip of his slipper (worn, the rounded toe jutting out). But he did not pull back his foot. He knew that he could not: now the spider was too close and he was caught in its sphere of immobile horror. So little is needed—So-and-So knew—to alarm a spider of that sort. All one had to do was breathe on it and it would, depending on the nearness of the enemy and his position, flatten itself against the floor, an immovable nailhead crowned by the billowing of its eight halo threads as by the thinnest jets of a fountain; or it would abandon itself as though dead with its threads in a cross and its belly (though where is the belly of that brown speck?) in the air, motionless and limp; or propped firmly on its threads (obviously equipped with suction cups), dangling from a wall or a web, it would begin a saraband with its hapless pepper-grain—an infernal, menacing whirl. Yet that spider gave no sign of being aware of So-and-So's presence, of his gaze and the breath he was holding, and, not at all alarmed, continued its fateful walk. It passed a half an inch away from So-and-So's toe, went forward and then disappeared in the direction of the deepest shadow and, perhaps, delirium. It was then that So-and-So roused himself and straightened up. His

mind was empty now, and he only felt a slightly feverish faint-
ness, he didn't actually feel sick. Maimed, broken inside. He
started back to bed, but as he turned to go his true nature
reawakened and he felt as always the absolute need to go back
in his mind over his relations with the spider race, as though to
fence off in space and time the danger which those terrible enemies meant for him. In his mind he pictured spiders of all sorts
and sizes: from those devourers of birds seen in books of natural
history (not dangerous, distant and unreal) to those miniscule
spiders with quivering palps which catch flies on window sills
(nor were they dangerous either: non-spiders).

There are many species of real spiders. There are the huge
old spiders, black as pitch, with a flat head and a heart-shaped
body; they live in old rooms and bear a large cross on their bodies,
have great stumpy, hairy legs and take frightful leaps. Squat,
corky spiders which, when one seizes them, contract their claws
around the clutching fingers. They live in gardens and do not
possess too furtive, conclusively swift and slippery a personality.
Then the spiders which are always seen as though through a
veil of mist, installed in holes at the end of a funnel of thick web.
Hearth crickets, which are very much like spiders (those which
So-and-So as a child used to call cricket-spiders). Medium-sized,
yellowish spiders without any definite characteristics, strangely
proportioned in their body and legs, neither squat nor lithe. . . .
"Yes," So-and-So said to himself at this point, following a
sudden thought, "but to catalogue them like this does not mean
to understand them. The flesh of spiders, the gloomy mystery
of spiderish flesh, is still denied us. Who can penetrate it, who
can know what it is really made of? So, one ought to study," he

went on, "those yellow spiders with legs too weak to support their distended bodies; which are nothing but a small blister of purulent matter: a small blister of sanies—bursting it, one sees a yellowish, thick liquid ooze out. As a matter of fact, the blister itself is not yellow, it is only transparent and colored by its contents. This is perhaps the essence of the spiders. That blister is like the skin of a very taut boil, a boil which absolutely must be pierced to make sure that the pus does not spread to the rest of the body. . . ." But here a flash ran through So-and-So's brain, heart and veins. As usual, only an instant later did he know what it was. The deadly agitation increased, reached the maximum bearable intensity, gave signs of diminishing and then began to assume the form of a thought, was embodied in a comparison. Another turn of the screw and then, fixed in all of its horror, the image. So-and-So understood. He understood now, suddenly, unexpectedly, the color of his son's eyes: the color of those spiders' bodies.

Here a strong stimulus called So-and-So to the place of his most recent glory and again he tried that supreme remedy. He ran to the toilet and, sitting down with dignity, declared: "I have called you here, sirs. . ." but his voice died out languidly and the contact with the imaginary audience was not established. The very stimulus proved to be fictitious: even So-and-So's body could no longer meet the situation: for it to be so refractory some essential harmony must have been disturbed.

By now So-and-So's condemnation was certain. Quietly he walked back into his room, dressed without haste and went out. As he crossed the courtyard—the heart of the house—the look he threw it was almost absent-minded.

5

El rojo pas de la blanca aurora

(Góngora)

. . .Mais la croix de l'aurore se casse et se ride. . .

Up there, snow on the mounatins, barely seen in the light
of the stars, and where was So-and-So going? He did not know
and he didn't care. He didn't care about anything. Familiar, rock-
strewn roads, rolling away beneath his random steps; then grassy
slopes. Then through the circle of the hills and even farther on,
through the passes first gentle, then steep. The contours of the
mountain ranges, the valleys. A wood-covered slope skirts a long
valley which comes to an end against the lofty sky. It is the hornbeam wood, the sacred refuge of the November woodcocks.
Black, gloomy hornbeam, as it is called. Snow, snow. Into the
woods. The light breeze, then the sparkling wind which rises
before the dawn. An east wind. And far off a faint, uncertain
brightness, a hint of pallor on the bluish transparent sky. Behind
him there is still the black pitch with just a touch of blue, and
everything grows dark, submerging itself in the night. An even
more somber night, since only the largest, reddest stars throb
mournfully and a waning moon, tragic and lopsided, russet and
sinister, looks like a sail fallen in a sudden calm. Undecided

whether to be terrorized by the diurnal danger which hovers imperceptibly on the horizon, the night looks at it askance as at a silly dog, holding its breath. Once again it seemed to So-and-So, who was following the path of the night, that he was in the depths of the sea and that the boundless slope of the sky was the surface of that sea, so far above his head: he had a sense of the immensity of the void beneath the hood of the sky, as if water filled it and rendered it palpable (the moon a pink jellyfish floating on the skin of the water, the stars starfish with their tenuous, swimming pulsation). Vertiginous fright. Yet an indefinable heightening, a surge of that distant brightness, brought him back to his senses.

Dark hornbeam. Few people, apart from hunters, know the dark hornbeam. The white hornbeam is bland and innocent, not much different from hazelnut; the dark ones have a grim, pertinacious, obstinate nature. They too bloom like all other plants and put forth leaves, but they do it perhaps in secret and no one has ever seen them bud and cover themselves with leaves. In all seasons a wood of dark hornbeam is nothing but a low underbrush, almost a tangled and knotty crawling along the ground. Solid as a stone, from which spring neat, very long withies, apparently flexible and hard as steel, in reality as slimy and prehensile as tentacles. It is not given us to know what particular mission the dark hornbeam is appointed to perform on this earth. But a reflection of its somber and impenetrable spirit discloses a sense of dread in whoever penetrates among that pearly people.

The hunter who attempts to open a path through a wood of dark hornbeam, not only inevitably leaves shreds of himself among the clawing knuckles of the roots and branches, and must not only struggle to free his shotgun a thousand times from a cluster of dry twigs which has mockingly seized it or grips it tightly like a dog clamps onto a bone; but the miserable creature, lost in the cosmic darkness and pearly entanglement of the shoots, must also, in order to get by, at every moment pull aside the lithe impudence of the withies. And at each instant the withies, tensed and strengthened for a second, hiss and beat down—precise and sure, gauged to the millimeter—on his frozen ears, the veined back of his hand, his cheeks, the skin beneath his eyes, on his quickly closed lids, on everything in him which is intimate and delicate. Having lashed out, often with its thinnest, most supple tip, the withy, as though nothing had happened, returns to its normal position and only a slight, indifferent swaying testifies to its furtive act. One does not know how it happens: in a thicket of other trees—let's even say of white hornbeam—a flexible branch which snaps back after having been bent, would at the most lash the person who comes after you. But here all amazement is quickly exhausted—as quickly as one exhausts all reserves of will. One becomes the prey of the spell cast by that airy and pearl-like, impudent and fierce people. Knotty gnomes and malicious sylphs, whose voice is that rustle and hiss, dance freely around in their wild saraband. The whiplash, without losing any of its biting twang, seems almost to linger and adhere to the flesh and often sounds like the fluttering of a woodcock's wings when, hindered by the underbrush, it rises in flight; it is but another mean trick which the wood plays on the hunter. And yet, even if the fluffy tuft of turtle-hued feathers swiveling on a sharp beak were at that moment to pass a yard away from the barrel of his shotgun, the hunter would dazedly let it go.

So-and-So had entered such a wood, but now he walked almost rapidly: the hornbeams must have realized his indifference, and the game mustn't have seemed too rewarding to them. Snow—which dawn has brightened a bit. Scratches, hisses and lashes run over his skin like the dull, constant roar of a torrent. Snow—but what is that white form which seems to leap from the snow and leap on the snow? There are completely white hares—a false, unheeded voice suggested to So-and-So. Too large and too small to be a hare. A lost sheep? the same voice insists, talking to itself. But it does not matter, for that white form which runs ahead of him, dawn-colored as the spider is the color of a gray shadow, seems to guide So-and-So. It races toward the brightness of the dawn.

Here begins that phase of the story which one might call the *horizontal walk,* and the writer, since his hero lacks awareness, is forced to peep through with his own coarse imagination. Everyone has seen that beautiful movie star walk with utter surrender toward redemption or love. Her eyes stare into the distance and her glance is completely horizontal; the obstacles, the asperities of the terrain are overcome and smoothed out, yet those eyes do not bend to look at them. The legs and body, softly, as though spellbound by the adamantine horizontality of that look, bend, stretch, twist and yield to the earth's surface of their own accord, so as not to disturb the inflexible direction of her desire. And if a branch or a trailing shawl hampers her step, if sand or swamp makes it drag, the instep and the shin and the knee, everything, will pull it along and conquer without feeling the weight, just so long as that eye remains free and that look swims straight above the entire world. Everyone has also seen Mickey Mouse riding blissfully on some baroque conveyance which stretches and shrinks in the most exaggerated fashion, and so gives the beast the sensation of riding on a wonderfully smooth road. Well, this is more or less how So-and-So was walking, his eyes fixed on that white shape. As in the movies. His feet sludged through the snow and stumbled over the knuckles of the roots, the withies struck down with a swish on his tenderest flesh, and the white shape, now close, now farther away, guided him toward the glow of dawn.

Until he fell down and lay there. Now the dawn was at its height, all things were trembling with drops, fresh, silvered, pearly: the stony slopes were dappled with silver. Beneath the jade sky the intertwined shoots, for an instant tamed and bewildered, seemed a forest of pearl-like and votive torches raised to the sky. Stretched out in the snow, So-and-So felt the cold penetrate deeper into his bones, his heart. And a malign shadow veined the dawn. The sky changed color, darkened with a yellow tinge. In front of So-and-So, through the tangle of branches, extended the white and immaculate valley: on one side the rounded flank of a mountain spur, which was also swelling and white with pure snow. Over that swelling the first light of dawn cast its yellow reflection: and the entire spur was transformed into the monstrous body of the spider. The kind of spider which has a small cluster of sanies for a body.

How long was So-and-So there, stretched out in the snow? Certainly the cold in his bones and heart was now ice, utter ice. Slow but sure, it liquified the last flickers of warmth and gripped, penetrating the skin. It penetrated and gripped. It gripped in an ever tighter vise which closed more and more rapidly, like the eye of a camera. Look, there is still a tiny point of light and heat, then—nothing more. As at the movies.

But by now what did those spiders matter to So-and-So? Indeed, it seemed to him that all of his resolutions had become an immense love and that he was tasting the deep-felt joy of a reconciliation with the ancestral enemy. At the same time an inner rumble warned him that something was taking place in his entrails: and a need resplendently materialized, a compelling, irresistible need: his lips colored with a weak smile.

Let the spidery flesh flourish!

Note: Here the writer believes that it is advisable, for a multiplicity of reasons one more intuitive than the next, to put a full stop. He will, just for the record, mention a circumstance which however does not seem essential to him. So-and-So—one later discovered—was not at all a sea captain, nor had he roamed the world encountering, as he claimed, the most astounding adventures. His life had been that of the usual poorly-paid clerk, right down to the day of his retirement. He had no relatives of any kind, and as for his little son, who later died of convulsions, at one time the usual nasty gossips had inferred that he was not his. Not content with that, they had gone about insinuating that the so-called captain (in fact, an assistant chief clerk in a ministerial department of the capital) was afflicted by a physical defect, so that he could not think of having sons or even women but only a very chaste wife. Chaste, of course, where he was concerned. How and when the captain had afterwards gone to live in the small town where we have found him, has been impossible to ascertain. As for Rosalba, who had been taken from an orphanage at the age of one, she managed to lure the lawyer's son so effectively that he, in the teeth of the usual ample advice of his parents, decided at all costs to marry her and since then the writer has lost sight of her.

But, as is quite clear, these are only negligible details.

Translated by Raymond Rosenthal

EDITOR'S NOTE: *The original title of this story was* W.C., *but since its first publication in the magazine* Caratteri *required something more rounded and extended, the present substitution was made, "but that is the death of the king of France" being a phrase one often hears applied to musical compositions that are long and wearisome.*

Giovanni and His Wife

T O BEGIN with, let us come to an agreement on what it means to be out of tune (vocally out of tune, that is—to simplify the discussion which, in any case, might hold for any kind of dissonance). To be out of tune does not apply, as is commonly believed, to someone who reproduces by singing, whistling or humming a song or musical phrase in an inexact fashion, departing more or less from the original score: at the most one could accuse such a person of a meager musical memory. Nor—I'll go so far as to say—does it apply to someone who, by his faulty reproduction, offends against the norms which by tradition and general consent regulate the relationships between sounds or groups of sounds. (Modern music could offer comfort to such a person!) To be out of tune applies only to those who each time that they repeat a song, repeat it always differently and always offend the above-mentioned norms and never (except by some inexplicable accident) adhere to the original score, it being understood, of course, that they are not aware of it and on the contrary are firmly convinced each time that they are reproducing the score to the letter. In short, to be out of tune consists precisely in the inability to have any sort of relationship with the score, or to establish a steady point of reference in the great tossing sea of sounds.

These introductory remarks were necessary for the exposition of the following case which, I believe, is unique in the story of relationships between people.

There was a certain man in our town (I shall call him Giovanni) who lived only for music. Especially for lyric or operatic music or whatever you wish to call it. It was also claimed that he was endowed with a singularly melodious and robust voice, and he himself said that he devoted all of his time to singing. It was claimed, I repeat, since Giovanni, who was rich and completely independent, not only didn't make the slightest effort to have a public career, but did nothing to share his precious gift with anyone else. Indeed, not even his friends had ever heard him sing. But, in recompense, everyone had heard him in the opera houses, learnedly discussing the capacity of one singer or another as well as this or that note and how it had been delivered.

I had not always known Giovanni well, but gradually we became more and more friendly and so, one fine day, yielding to my reiterated insistence, he decided to grant me a concert in his house, which I had not yet been to. When I arrived there I quickly understood the reason for his constant reserve, as the reader will also immediately understand.

Giovanni had a wife, whom I now saw, a woman of great

beauty and suavity. She was, so it seemed, very devoted to him. Blonde and very young, indeed almost a girl, and from a family which was without a doubt at least as noble as his own.

After having taken our places in the drawing room where the grand piano was located, Giovanni asked me to select a few from among the many arias—all from very well known operas—which he felt he knew best. So I selected some of those which were most familiar to me, in order to appreciate his art more fully, and then Giovanni, with his wife accompanying him, began to sing.

I was dumbfounded, unable at first to believe my own ears. In the exordium (it was the popular recitative from *Aida* which begins with the words *Se quel guerriero io fossi...*) I did not recognize a single note, nor could I grasp a single consecutive bar. Now, don't misunderstand me: it was not a matter here of the common off-key singing, ranging from a quarter to half a tone, to which amateur singers and people singing on the street have more or less accustomed us. It was a real jamboree of capriciously clashing sounds, which, believe me, not only had no relation whatsoever to the score but also did not bear the slightest relation to each other.

I had no reason to think that my memory of the tune had failed me, and besides, the accompaniment was there and must have meant something. I could do nothing but hope that my friend was following his personal counterpoint and that this would eventually establish a firm relationship between the notes of the score and those emitted by him. Alas, I soon realized that any given note of the score was always matched by a different note in the singing. And even calling them notes is a bit too much: they were something intermediate or adulterated which cannot be found in nature, that is, on the keyboard. Even if I had wished to judge those bellows as something entirely independent from the score—as an original composition or improvisation—I would have been immediately undeceived by a resumption of the melody (let us call it that), when from those lips, prettily pursed and almost smiling, issued sounds which were not only discordant and lacerating but brand-new. Giovanni's voice in itself was not at all harsh or insipid; and yet, used so badly, it could not help but be disagreeable.

After the first piece Giovanni absently asked me for my opinion and before I could reply he had started another, then a third, a fourth. . . . I had to be careful to hide my reactions since, as he sang, he kept looking at me.

At last, to bring their hospitable courtesy to a worthy close, he asked his wife to perform a few duets with him, including some ensemble singing, and she graciously consented. And here a new, unimaginable surprise awaited me, indeed the greatest surprise of the evening. It is hardly a matter for wonder, it is even completely natural that a person who sings out of tune, if he has no way of checking on himself, does not know that he is singing out of tune. But what follows is truly a matter for amazement.

I must explain that, during the entire exhibition, I had assiduously observed the young wife's face, trying to determine what she thought of all this, and all that I had seen was the rapt expression with which she continued to gaze at her husband. This, however, did not seem to imply a definite opinion. Now, as soon as she opened her mouth, I immediately realized that she sang as much out of tune as he did. And that wasn't all—and this is the astounding part—she sang out of tune precisely and identically in his fashion, as if to his direction, according to his inspiration, his mode, no matter how varying and momentary. I am at a loss to add anything else.

If I had needed proof, I would have been supplied with incontrovertible evidence by the "duo" of this first duet, and then by the others which followed. Well, he who wishes to refer back to the introductory remarks which I have set at the beginning of this story, will easily understand that two people who sing out of tune cannot, by definition, sing *together,* except by mere chance and for a single note, at least a single note at a time. Yet these two unfailingly agreed on each and every note, or whatever you might call them, and they sang entire pieces with such moving accord in their out-of-tuneness that I, amazed, consternated, dejected, let my shapely ears be lacerated almost willingly, meanwhile abandoning myself to philosophical reflections, half bitter, half comforting.

I can imagine the objection that will be raised. Could it not have been that although she was aware of how matters stood, out of an excess of devotion and so as not to hurt her husband, the woman was trying not to disillusion him and was making an effort to follow him in his distortions, proving by this that she possessed an especially subtle ear? But, leaving aside my presence, which would have frustrated such a plan, who, even among the most expert of singers, could have succeeded in reproducing the sounds emitted by Giovanni, which, as I have already said, bore no relation at all to the universally known notes and, during their emission, were continually different and varied? Besides, the seriousness and gravity with which she went about her singing was by no means ambiguous.

When all had ended, the moment came to express my opinion, and this time Giovanni stared straight in my face so that I would be forced to reveal my innermost feelings. Shifting nervously, as on a bed of thorns, how I managed I don't quite know, but I proferred the conventional compliments and got out of that house as fast as I could. He, however, was not deceived by my gracious words, for afterwards he barely answered my greeting, thus showing that he was not even touched by doubts as to the excellence of his art. Then we lost sight of each other altogether.

That evening, as I was going home, I brooded over the obscure designs of nature's cruelty which instills in one person a vivid passion for the things which he cannot do, while it fills another with dislike for those things he can do very well, and so on. Yet nature is also benevolent, because with one hand it gives back that which it has taken with the other (though one does not see why it took it away in the first place). After all, weren't those two perfectly happy? Of their incapacity, nearly segregated from the world as they were, they had not the slightest suspicion and thus could, with the purest bliss, far from any menace, give themselves up to their passion—so true is it that our real abilities do not at all make up the substance of our existence. And one would have to prove that theirs was indeed an incapacity in the absolute sense. So I came to the definite conclusion that they were not only *not* humiliated but rather openly favored by fate—with which I was therefore for the moment reconciled.

However, this thread of thoughts then lacked an end which fell into my hands recently although I had lost all memory of Giovanni and everything connected with him. I heard that his young wife had suddenly died: she had burst a vein in her breast while singing. So Giovanni has in his turn been plunged into the gloomiest grief. And while waiting to tie together these far-reaching reflections, nothing remains for us but to adopt the explanation of the poet: Giovanni can quite well say of himself and his Annabel Lee:

> "But we loved with a love that was more than love—
>   I and my Annabel Lee—
> With a love that the winged seraphs in Heaven
>   Coveted her and me.
>
> And this was the reason that, long ago,
>   In this kingdom by the sea,
> A wind blew out of a cloud, chilling
>   My beautiful Annabel Lee. . . ."

Let us hope that he may at least find the consolation—for some persons insufficient—that is mentioned further on in the poem.

Translated by Raymond Rosenthal

Sunstroke

L'éloquence ne tord pas son cou.

SUDDENLY the owl slackened her flight and alighted on a forked branch: a sense of tedium, a vague discomfort had begun to overcome her. Not that the dawn had begun to whiten the sky, though it was beginning to push up behind the horizon and the stars had grown a little pale to the east. The uproarious day was approaching, and a touch of brightness already veiled the most distant peaks from the owl's eyes. There was no doubt: the baleful sun was loping like a wolf and soon would appear in greedy triumph behind the ridges.

The owl's nausea and melancholy grew in response to the unrolling of that arc of sky, which carried with it that shadow of light. Now the east was already whitening and the feral pallor was spreading by imperceptible tremors. The dead turn white, and so does the night that dies. And now a benumbing sound, not yet fully uttered, dully swarmed at the valley's borders: the voice of the light getting ready to scream its clangorous tumult.

The first murmur of the leaves erupted in the breeze, while the whiteness became more pronounced, impregnating the curtains of the air. The song of the first bird arose with a crash; it went on alone for a while, then other voices joined it, the chorus swelled. From this moment on it overflowed without check, rising from a murmur to a hum, a swarming and then a din. The olive trees turned silver, and then the sky, the wind, the clouds; they all became golden, and veiled themselves in blood. The dust of emeralds and jade swayed in the heights, and the coral dust of the cirrus. But at each instant an arcane fire blew over the faded mists and lit them up, transforming them into vivid slopes. In unison with the din, the day acclaimed itself.

Shrill chirpings, impatient moans lifted to meet the on-coming sun: the encircling shadows fled, and the last creatures of the night. Against this adverse element the owl shrank into herself, dismayed, and already the contours of things had blurred. She felt lost, because the tide poured roaring into her; she could not fight this and was compelled to seek her last refuge. Just as man in the shadows of night still preserves in the deepest part of himself a last flicker, a spark of light, so in the unleashed day the owl keeps lit the fire of darkness. But some-times the small fire flickers, the spark threatens to go out, the shadows teem up like whirlpools of subterranean water from some dark gorge; or the darkness grows pale and in its place spread the light and din.

The sun was pressing through the crests of the mountains and, set in the sky, it looked like a luminous boil—which soon, in a moment, would burst. The owl waited with contracted lids for its loss of darkness. A long moment passed; it seemed incredible that the boil should last that long—the skin of the sky must surely split, it was so taut and shiny. And yet it still stretched and became even shinier, without bursting. An infinite gap of anguish—when a frightening evil threatens us, let it at least come quickly, so that we can throw ourselves into its arms!

The crested lord of the day suddenly emerged with a crash, quickly towering over the arid expanses of rock. Then the final dread overwhelmed the owl and blindness surrounded her. And with his appearance, the horde of ignoble courtiers began singing his praises with greater boldness; and his handmaidens, the lights and colors, began to sway, to flow, to dance, The purplish mists, the night's residue, scattered, putting up a last despairing struggle. But the presence of the master instilled courage and arrogance in that whole pack of slovenly solar beings. Oh shameless roar, oh unleashed clashing of water, oh reeling of lightrays, of boughs, of leaves! At that moment you thought yourselves the masters of the earth, and of all the creatures of the woods, the air and sea! You are fat, proud progeny now, but when time has run out for your heavenly satyr, he will plunge sheerly behind the mountains or into the salty depths, and other somber, brown shadows will regain mastery over the world.

But this is the end for the owl. The roar deafens her, the flashes and glare blind her; she will die from this light and this din. Disheartened and hopeless, her eyes staring, she tries vainly to see through the agitated brightness and sways and sighs on her branch. None of the diurnal beings notice her and her muted sigh is swallowed by the air.

The clangor and the dazzle gather and grow compact. The shrieks and flashes are unbearable; ever more vivid, ever louder; tongues, blades of bellowing fire. They grow even more intense; and the flashes no longer flash but are a single flash, dilating fixed, immense and blinding, an intolerable, lacerating sight! The roar, the shriek is a howl, a yowl; high and swollen it fills the hollow of the sky. The fearful blacksmith of the day—and one can no longer tell whether it is light, sound or heat—hammers burningly at the eyes and entrails; the universe blazes up. The heart pounds frantically in the death agony.

A shot, a blinding, incandescent flare; the roar subsides into a hum and ceases; the owl plunges into the white light of death.

"Well, how do they work?"

"Eh, I'd thought they didn't have enough gunpowder in them! Don't you see? It dropped down alive. I'll have to doctor these cartridges."

But although she still fluttered there on the ground before a dog which was sniffing her suspiciously, and perhaps still tried feebly to fly, the owl no longer knew what was happening and was happy.

"Aren't you going to pick it up?"

"What would I do with it?"

Translated by Raymond Rosenthal

A Romantic's Letter on Gambling

To the memory of Châli
18. .

DEAR Ignazio:

Gambling, yes gambling! And who would dare to reproach me for it? This life is mine! It is true, my nights are burnt away, my days are shut off from the sun and the gambols of the air; indeed they are spent in torpor and sleep. So what? May the envious sun perish and forever submerge in the ether's gurgling abyss and a perpetual night stretch its wings over us. "Praised be the eternal night, praised be the eternal sleep." But not the sleep, the nocturnal fever, the dark passions which rend and curse us, and among these darkest and most ardent, most sinister and sacred, the unquenchable fire of the shadows—divine and infernal gambling! Who would dare to be the first to re-

proach me? And why should I justify myself by pointing to my
miserable life? Even if I were the greatest of the earth's great
and in my heart there shone a perennial springtime, even if I
were peaceful and happy, I would still deny all earthly and
heavenly fortune and willingly, indeed with disdain, throw
them at the feet of that somber deity! Here great destinies are
decided, here man, no longer alone but in his true country,
amidst a thousand other fearful beings, awaits the touch of the
hand which will lift him up or lay him low; here man does not
pretend to be a creator, does not expect to attain his damnation
or salvation by means of his mediocre anguish. Here he, utterly
a creature, solicits, almost like the chalice of a flower open to the
gifts and offenses of the sky, an immediate response, prepared
to rebel, prepared to worship, prepared (if he is a real man) to
worship even when struck down. And yet—miracle of grace—
there is, unfathomable decree, something heroic in this situation:
here blows the broad, voracious wind of the spaces which dis-
perses the mean worries, the contemptible, tedious compromises;
here for one instant king and emperor, the next instant a worm
in the earth, the scion of man whether overwhelmed or triumphant, is in either case overwhelmed and therefore triumphant,
if he bows his head to the will of heaven with a pure heart. Here
he, struck by religious awe, lives his gravest hours; here, at last,
Adventure and Mystery, those supreme gifts of Providence, act
out their free drama. So let us praise gambling, the highest
activity of the human spirit!

But even if it were true, Ignazio, all that the petty whisper
about this noble passion of the soul, in which man stakes himself
with all his being and dignity; even if it were true what the

uninitiated and fearful whisper, what can I do against that which ravishes me? Is it perhaps my fault, my dear friend, if of all the good God's gifts which you list in your letter I can enjoy none unless I have pacified this devouring thirst, this anxiety, which swells within me and grows beyond all bounds, and demands ever new nourishment, almost like a monstrous animal nestling in my bowels, a cancer which sucks all my vital lymph? And, observe, it is the other face of the blissful or blissless mystery that there should be only one way to placate this surging wish—to lose. Years ago I even worked out a theory about this, about the ineluctable plot of which I am the victim. I will try to explain it to you. In the first place you ought to know that the world offers me nothing pleasant and tolerable if it is not connected in some way with this passion: wherever I go I have the secret hope of feeding it, whomever I approach I have the secret hope of convincing him to gamble with me. In short, by now I conceive of all existence in terms of gambling and it would seem emptier than it does if gambling were taken from me (so do not curse it: it helps me to live). Now, you speak of the rays of the sun, of the flights of the swallows, of kittens. Very well, these sights and impressions are perhaps so many blessings from heaven; but how could one—I have long been asking myself anxiously—how could one enjoy them, just like that, for themselves (though you seem to be able to)? How could one, if not in relation to something else, something different, their opposites? Provided, of course, you really love them. Or, if I must use the words consecrated by the vulgar, how can a pure man enjoy purity and a sinner sin? For example, I, a sinner, enjoy the purity which is gambling. In short, what I mean to say is that only to

him who comes out of the infernal abyss can the stars look
virginal. But bear with me while I tell you something of myself—
perhaps I'll be able to be clearer, but don't try to catch me in a
contradiction.

I was in Venice; heavy velvet drapes had been closed over
the windows against the invasion of the light of day and the
first rays of the sun: the men intent around the oblong table
reject every light but that of the low-hanging lamp. But I was
forced to leave: I had lost everything, everything down to the
last small coin, and I had no hopes from any quarter, I no longer
dared look for help from anyone. I was alone and foresaken in a
strange city, and lost forever—at least that's what I thought.

I walked out onto the driveway in the dawn and sat down
on a bench. Ignazio, if the unconquerable force which had
dragged me along all night and had compelled me to caress that
soft skin, the green felt, was impure, how could it now have been
replaced by such a wonderful feeling of peace, a grave and
dreamy serenity, a quiet, full enchantment? Never as then had
I felt so conscious of myself and yet so wedded and merged with
the elements. Never so tranquilly had the world opened up to
me in harmonious appearances, in placid forms and features, yet
rich with inner, radiant life, with promises and—I say it without
hesitation—with hope. Above my head, alone, a little bird
chirped in a calm tone, not vied with by any other voice, indeed
supported by the subdued drone of the morning breeze among
the leaves, through whose fringe the first incarnate rays of the
sun were already playing. The sky and sea were both immaculate, each according to its fashion; the gravel of the

driveway gleamed. Already by imperceptible throbs the thousand inhabitants of the earth swarmed all around; but above all rose that solitary, aerial voice. And it seemed the voice of the entire benumbed world, heavy with sleep in the dawn of its existence, when for the first time it awakens under the divine touch of the eternal; it sounded to me, Ignazio, like the very voice of the age of innocence. I was lost in that Eden, all excitement had by now left me and I wasn't even striving for a lofty calm, for it was in me and pervaded me unbeknownst to myself; and I was a part of those dispersed yet fraternal elements. I was, finally, happy.

Later, on the lagoon, the boat caught up with and passed a gondola which was gliding alone, at a distance from the shore. It bore an old woman of noble aspect, who was quietly talking with the gondolier, and a young girl of great and shy beauty who, resting her elbows on her knees and her chin on the palms of her hands, gazed into the distance with an air of marvelous melancholy: We slowly left that gondola behind, and I did not even desire that she, the young girl, suddenly rousing herself from her dream, should extend her hand over the lagoon and say: "Look, I was waiting for you." I enjoyed her even though she vanished and I shall never see her again, and not for a single moment did I desire more than had been granted me. For it seemed to me that even in this way she belonged to me, just as that entire morning did: I was no longer "I" but every other thing, or rather myself and at the same time in every other thing, and every other thing, while being itself, was me. And I had no desires, but not because I had an empty heart; indeed it over-

flowed with all that is good, and every desire was fulfilled at the
very moment I felt it. I cannot explain to you what it was—it is
so much easier to describe desperation than happiness. But I
know and say to you that that morning I believed and prostrated
myself in spirit to the Creator, and for the first time I thanked
him for the life he had given me, for the world which he had
composed around me, and for all the riches that it offers us,
provided our good will might only know how to conquer them.
The man who should have felt miserable and deserted and
anxious, thanked the Creator; the man who was not sure of living, thanked Him for the life which could still be taken from
him; the man who should have raised his fists in imprecation
against heaven, worshipped—how do you explain this, Ignazio?
I thanked Him also for having freed me.

But now I have come to the crux. Freed from what? Was
not perhaps the secret and powerful surge of the evening before,
the swelling of my passion, His work too? And why does He
condemn His creatures (or only me?)not to enjoy His gifts
unless they have first scorned or lost them? Why can one not
enjoy any one thing unless one has gone through something
else much different or even utterly opposed? Listen to me,
Ignazio, could all this be blasphemy? And if, as I do believe, in
the universal plot there is always to be found a swelling or
tumescence followed by a detumescence or contraction; if every
living thing (and thus everything) is subject to this fatal alter-
nation; if it is wise to endure the swelling in order to achieve
the lofty calm, and if for the one the other is an inescapable
condition—shall we not admit the divine origin of that swelling,
too? Even though it might represent the tangle of evil in contrast

to the calm unfolding of good? Who would dare to deny its necessity, who could even prove the pre-eminence of the second experience?

I know that I should never have pronounced these words. Forgive me, Ignazio, I will not trouble you any more. But some other time perhaps I shall praise for you the cards themselves, those humble yet ethereal instruments of divine decisions. Have you ever looked at them? Some impassive and vivid, others diverse, others radiant, gay and silky like the skin of a woman, they figure immemorial tales, primordial legends. They embroider and adorn the depths of my nights just as the sagas of the North or the fairy tales of the Orient adorn the glittering shadow of childhood! Oh blessed petals fallen from the mystic rose! Oh vital and mortal dew! But this time I'm trying to amuse you. Addio, etc.

(signature)

Translated by Raymond Rosenthal